BENEATH
THE
WATERS

Novels By Oswaldo França, Júnior, Available In English

THE MAN IN THE MONKEY SUIT
THE LONG HAUL
BENEATH THE WATERS

BENEATH THE WATERS

OSWALDO FRANÇA JÚNIOR

Translated by Margaret A. Neves

BALLANTINE BOOKS · NEW YORK

An Available Press Book
Published by Ballantine Books

Translation Copyright © 1990 by Margaret A. Neves

All rights reserved under International and Pan-American Copyright Conventions. Published in the United States by Ballantine Books, a division of Random House, Inc., New York, and simultaneously in Canada by Random House of Canada Limited, Toronto. Originally published in Portuguese as *No Fundo Das Aguas* by Editora Nova Fronteira S/A in 1987. Copyright © 1987 by Jacyra Fonseca França.

Library of Congress Catalog Card Number: 89-92112

ISBN: 0-345-36461-9

Cover design by Bill Geller
Cover photograph: The Image Bank/© 1985 Peter Grey
Text design by Holly Johnson
Manufactured in the United States of America
First American Edition: February 1990
10 9 8 7 6 5 4 3 2 1

*For Ana
and Arlete*

BENEATH THE WATERS

When the floodgates of the dam were closed, everyone had already abandoned their homes and lands, never to return. It had all been planned. The waters rose slowly, reaching the street next to the riverbank first. In this street lived Dona Graciema, who grated manioc root and toasted it to make the best manioc flour you could find in the region. Her husband was called José Júlio, and his work was building and repairing the copper stills on the plantations that produced rum. Next door to Dona Graciema and José Júlio lived Dona Zulmira, a seamstress, and her husband, Cristiano, who used to be a horsebreaker until the day he was thrown from the saddle and knocked his head against the heavy post of a farm gate. Then he couldn't ride anymore because of dizzy spells, so he began to work with a string of burros. But he became absentminded and went around with his fly open, leaving the burros forgotten on the road, neglecting to speak to people, and Dona Zulmira convinced him to stay home and take care of the garden. She began taking in more sewing and watched him as he cultivated the plants. When she made clothes for her friends and acquaintances, she was careful that he didn't go outside without a shirt, barefoot, or with his fly open. Cristiano took care of the garden, watering and weeding it, inspecting the plants leaf by leaf for fungi, plant lice, pests.

He dug new beds and seeded them. Two or three times a week he picked lettuce, cabbage, watercress, put it in a basket, and went out to sell it.

Dona Zulmira would make him put on a decent shirt, check to be sure he had shoes on and his fly zipped, give him a cap for his head, and say, "All right, you can go."

He would walk off with the basket over his arm and usually he came back without any money, for he gave the vegetables away for free to the girls with longer hair and skirts that showed off their knees. They enchanted him, and he didn't charge them anything.

He would come back with his basket empty and when Dona Zulmira asked him, "Did you sell everything, Cristiano? Where's the money?" he would answer, "I gave the stuff to the girls."

Dona Zulmira didn't mind. He didn't even go so far as to talk with the girls, just stared at them, enchanted, and offered the things he grew for free. During the hotter part of the year, he got into the habit of going into the bedroom and undressing. Dona Zulmira kept the windows and door of the living room and kitchen locked so that he wouldn't go out in the garden and also so he couldn't be seen from the street. Their daughter, called Chandina, lived nearby and helped to keep an eye on him when her mother needed to deliver some sewing or buy notions. And if she saw him coming out of the room naked, she would warn him, "Don't go around like that, Father, go put some clothes on."

Obediently, he would go back to the bedroom, but at times he would come out again with only a shirt on.

"Father, you forgot your trousers."

He would return and put them on. Chandina's husband

was called Urbano and they had two children, a boy and a girl. Nicolas was three, and Lenita was only a six-month-old baby. Chandina would take them both along when her mother called her to keep an eye on her father. She and Urbano lived next door to the house of a man known as Zé Gato, who people said had had lands, cows, and farms but had gambled everything away on the countless occasions he had gotten drunk and decided to play cards. All he had left was a horse that had been given back to him when he lost his last piece of land. The horse was white and answered to the name of Champion, and he was the thing Zé Gato cared most about. Every afternoon, Zé Gato washed and brushed his coat, gave him corn and carrots to eat, and sometimes a piece of brown sugar. He would do this even when he was out on the ranches round about buying beef cattle for Mr. Teodoro's slaughterhouse. It was common for him to ride around half-groggy, drowse off, and fall out of the saddle. Then Champion would stop and wait until he hit the ground. And until Zé Gato got up, he wouldn't leave the place. His horseshoes had cleats in the front and the thinner part in the back, because Zé Gato always believed that he was being pursued, and that way whoever was chasing him would think he was going away when in fact he was approaching. Pompeia, his wife, didn't like Champion one little bit. It wasn't just on account of the time her husband dedicated to taking care of him, it was also because the horse represented the loss of their last piece of land.

"That horse will be your ruin," she would predict.

One day, when he least expected it, she set out to kill

him with a scythe. "He'll drag you by one stirrup when you're falling down drunk out on these roads!"

But Zé Gato didn't listen to her. He trusted Champion and believed that he would stay by his side to protect him from his enemies when he fell asleep and slipped out of the saddle.

Near the house of Zé Gato and Pompeia lived Osmar, who was a digger of cisterns and had worked in a place very far away, in Mato Grosso, cleaning and preparing land for pasture. The wages were so low that he couldn't even buy food, and he had to run away through the forest with only the clothes on his back. He had seen a companion try to quit and go away, but the men in charge of the workers went after him and brought him back beaten and bloody. They warned that anyone who wanted to leave had to pay what he owed in the company canteen first. The man who tried to run away made a second attempt and they went after him again with dogs. When they got back, they told what they had done to him. They had left him in the forest after beating him and running a wooden stake up his anus.

"If hunger doesn't finish him off, the fever and infection will take care of him soon enough," they said.

Nevertheless Osmar decided to leave and made his preparations. He got together a knife, fish hooks, a line, matches, and rolled them all up in a plastic bag, which he tied to his waist. On a very dark, moonless night he ran off into the forest. The men didn't catch him. He walked for sixteen days until he found a road. He was thin and weak, but he got to the road and followed it to a city, where he found work as an assistant cistern digger. After staying for a while, he left that job and traveled around here and there.

He went to the river, got on a boat, and came to the place where the waters of the dam would one day cover everything. And he worked making cisterns, got to know people, found a girlfriend. He ended up falling in love with a girl called Lili who had a crippled leg, and they married and had five children. Only when his acquaintances started talking about life's hardships and troubles did he remember the place in Mato Grosso and the sixteen days in the jungle.

The house where Osmar lived with Lili and their five children was right besides Josilton's. Before Josilton was thirty-two years old he was the father of seven. Much later, when he and his wife, Jusciléia, thought no more children would come, she got pregnant. And Salome was born, a small-boned quiet baby girl who hardly cried. She became Josilton's passion. He had never cared to play with the other children or paid them much attention, but with Salome it was different. He liked to be near her anytime, to carry her, amuse her. He worked as a carpenter, and when he went to build a shed on a ranch about half a mile from town, Jusciléia sent their youngest boy, Danilo, eleven, to deliver his father's lunch. Josilton didn't like that; he said she should have brought it herself, and Salome too. So Jusciléia lined a big basket with a cloth, put the little girl in it, and took her along to deliver the lunch. Josilton stopped working and watched Salome as he ate. Afterward he held her in his arms, played with her a few minutes, and put her back in the basket. Then Jusciléia took her home again. She arrived worn out and behind with her other tasks, but it had to be that way because Josilton couldn't bear not to see the little girl. One day when the shed was almost built she arrived carrying Salome and the lunch and saw Josilton fighting with the driver who delivered the lumber. The driver was called Adriano and he owned the wagon and two teams of oxen. He had a piece of board in his hand and was beating Josilton over the head. Josilton had a piece of wood, too, trying to defend himself, and hit his opponent. Josilton's head was all bloody. When Jusciléia saw him like that, she screamed and dropped the lunch, grabbed Salome from the basket, and ran home again. There she stayed, crying and saying that the driver was killing Josilton, a father with eight children to raise, and one of them brand new. When her husband came home with his head bandaged up in a rag that afternoon, she was still crying and complaining.

"Shut up, woman," he told her.

A man arrived and they both went out back where Josilton was fattening some pigs. And they made a trade: a pig for a muzzle-loading pistol. Josilton started going around armed, and one day he spied Adriano leaving the riverbank with his wagon and two teams of oxen.

Josilton followed from a distance and, when they were well out of town, pulled out the pistol and shouted, "Your time has come, thief!"

Adriano jumped to the other side of the ox cart and hid behind a wheel. Josilton went around, trying to aim the pistol at him. Adriano, crouching down, ducked behind the oxen. They went round and round the ox cart and the animals, which calmly made their way down the road, until Josilton fired a shot. The bullet hit the leg of one of the oxen in the rear team. It was a black ox, which began kicking when it took the shot.

Adriano saw where the bullet had gone and screamed,

"Ah, you son of a bitch, so you want to kill my ox, eh?" He came after Josilton with his whip. The pistol was a muzzle-loader, and there wasn't time for Josilton to reload it. So he turned and ran, with Adriano pursuing him, cursing and trying to slash him with the whip. Josilton fled toward the river and stayed hidden for several days. He would come home very late and leave very early through the kitchen door. Much later, when they were building the bandstand in front of the church, Juscileia, arriving with her husband's lunch and Salome, saw Adriano's ox cart next to the building site. Anxious, she drew slowly near and saw Josilton and Adriano beside a man who was unloading boards and shingles. They were both examining what the man was unloading from the cart, at times almost touching but without addressing one another. They were doing business, but they addressed only the man who was unloading the wagon. Each as if the other didn't exist, wasn't present.

When the waters reached Josilton's house, they began to cover the last houses of that street near the riverbank: those of João Luis, Ronam, and Quirino. João Luis manufactured bricks with the kiln that had belonged to his father, a very industrious man by the name of Agostinho, but known to everyone as Lard. He died when a mud bank caved in on top of him. People called him Lard because he had dealt in pork lard before he was married. He would go door-to-door through the streets crying his wares. João Luis had always helped his father in the brick kiln, and after the father died, he became its owner. A thin man, he was known as Lard's João.

Quirino, another man who lived at the end of the street, was the owner of a small grocery. Of his five children, Tulio and Victor, the two oldest, went to school in the morning and in the afternoon helped him over the counter. Tulio, who was twelve, liked birds and had taught a blackbird to eat berries. When he came home from school, he would hang the cage among the branches of a berry bush in the backyard and the blackbird would peck at the berries within reach. Victor, eleven, was very business-minded. He had a he-goat and four nannies and he also raised fighting cocks. When he got home from school, he would cut grass for the goats, take care of the cocks, and then have lunch. Afterward he would lead the nanny goats out and tether them where they could graze. From the counter he listened attentively to the braying of these four female goats and their kids. While he waited on customers and controlled the goat herd, he would be arranging for the sale or barter of fighting cocks and also negotiating the kids that had completed two months of age. He always had money in his pocket. His father complained of the boy's mania for doing business, but when he needed money to complete some payment or other, he went to the boy for loans. And Victor always gave him the loans, at interest.

Ronam, whose house was the last on the street, had a wagon with rubber tires and a burro. He transported what the boatmen bought and sold. He would haul squashes, manioc root, unrefined sugar, cotton, and even chickens from the boats to the warehouses. And bolts of cloth, cans of kerosene, rolls of wire, and bags of salt from the warehouses to the boats. In the wagon bed, resting against rubber strips, he kept some sheets of zinc, which bounced as the wagon moved. He used them to put under the tires and keep the wagon from getting stuck on the sandy river beach.

After coming up to the street near the bank, the waters continued rising and covered other streets and other places farther away, like Miguel's ranch house, which was on a slope. From his veranda, Miguel could see the corral to the left, the foreman's house to the right, and directly ahead, a beautiful valley with pastures and an enormous *jequitibá* tree. Women were always getting pieces of its bark to make tea when they had menstrual problems. Early one morning, a bolt of lightning hit the tree trunk. Miguel was on the veranda at the time, observing the heavy clouds that were forming over the valley. When the lightning flashed, he heard a sharp report, and it was as if an ax had suddenly split the immense tree apart from top to bottom. Miguel saw the heavy branches falling, broken loose, and the trunk cracking in two. The cows that were near the tree fell to the ground. He and some of his employees went up close to take a look. They found the cows dead, each in a different position. There were twelve of them and they all had their tongues sticking out, necks bent, and eyes open. Dead, every last one. Miguel sent his workers to fetch their relatives and friends. He told them to go off down the roads announcing to everyone thereabouts that he was giving away meat. Crowds of people came. Out in the rain that lasted all day long, the workers butchered the cows, cut the meat into pieces, and distributed them generously. Each person took as much as he wanted and there was still a lot left over. On the ground they left the shanks, chest meat, necks. The filet mignon, which they said was unsubstantial meat and didn't give one strength. The lungs, the internal parts. Next day the vultures began to descend early. They came from far away, in such bands they looked like clouds, and covered what was left of the cows, picking the bones clean. For a week people still came up to the gates, asking if this was the place where a bolt of lightning had killed many cows and they were giving away the meat.

The workers would point to the clean-picked bones on the ground and say, "What's left is over there."

The waters covered these lands and also those of a man called Rodolfo, who was a good son and a good brother, but was very fond of women. He had three ranches and one of his neighbors, Sinésio Silva, became a widower. Sinésio went into town and got Janice, a young girl who worked in the red-light zone, and took her to live on his ranch. He put her in a house that he had built near a cave and every night went to visit her. The girl was pretty and had two little children. Rodolfo had already visited her once in the town, and when he found out she was there on Sinésio Silva's land, he began to go out of his way to pass the house. He would ride past the gate and look at Janice wearing shorts, washing clothes at the tap, plucking chickens, sweeping the back porch. She worked with her pretty legs unhampered, legs he already knew. But she didn't lift her face or look in his direction. Once she turned around and saw him on his horse. He tipped his hat in greeting.

"Hello there, Janice."

She smiled and lowered her face again. He went home extremely pleased, and the next time he stopped outside the fence he commented, "How pretty you look."

She didn't answer, only smiled again. The third time

Janice looked in his direction, he asked if she would invite him in for some coffee.

"That wouldn't be a good idea, Rodolfo. It wouldn't be right," she commented.

The fact that Janice had spoken his name gave Rodolfo new hope, and next time she responded to his greeting, he tied the horse to a tall stump, climbed under the fence wire, and went to the kitchen door. They talked a little, laughed a lot, and he tried to hug her, but Janice wouldn't let him.

She drew back, saying, "Go on, get away from here."

He went away and on the next day greeted her again. She answered him, he tied up the horse, went under the fence, and after they had talked a while he began kissing her.

"Don't do this," she said. "You'll wreck my life."

Rodolfo closed the door of the kitchen so the children who were playing in the backyard couldn't come in, took her to the bedroom, and they made love. When they were finished, she got up quickly and began pushing him outside.

"Get out of here, go away," she said. Looking at him, she repeated, "You'll wreck my life."

Rodolfo began to spend all his time thinking about meeting her again. He knew the horses Sinésio Silva rode and would watch from a distance to see if he was with Janice or not. Once she commented, "Sinésio asked if you had been by here."

"What did you tell him?"

"I told him no, and that even if you had gone past on the road, I wouldn't know because I'm not sure who you are." Rodolfo became worried. One afternoon there was no horse in sight and he went up to the house, but he noticed Sinésio Silva in the living room, passing in front of the window. Rodolfo rode away, and after that he changed his tactics. He started to watch every morning for Sinésio Silva to go out, following him until he was sure he really wasn't coming back.

"You can't come here anymore," Janice told him. "Sinésio suspects something."

"Oh, that's just your imagination," Rodolfo answered. "He never saw me around here."

So he kept on visiting her. Whenever he went back to the ranch where he lived, he would stop off to see his parents. His father was seventy-nine and his mother seventy-eight. They lived alone, and one night, when it was time to leave, he went to the kitchen to say good-bye to his mother.

"Your blessing. I'm going now," he said.

She was cooking some porridge and asked him to wait until his father had finished taking his bath.

"He's been having dizzy spells lately and I worry."

Rodolfo waited until his father came out of the bathroom, sat on the bed, and watched him eat his porridge. It was a porridge his mother prepared every night, with lots of milk and pieces of cheese. He accepted some from a bowl and said good-bye. He didn't stay longer because the next day he had to get up early to separate some heifers that Nathan, his oldest son who worked with him, was going to take to another ranch called Mother of Mankind. There was a moon in the sky and the night was very bright. He remembered this clearly, because when he stopped on a rise near a gate, about two miles from his house, some dark clouds covered the moon. He had been thinking about the pastures, which were dry, and those clouds were a sign that the rains would not be long in coming. When he bent over to lift the gate latch, he heard a shot ring out from the forest. He knew that sound well: it was the weak report of a store-bought cartridge. That same instant he felt lead entering his arm and blood spilling out.

He screamed an expression his mother had taught him to say in times of danger: "Holy Virgin, protect me!"

As he cried out he stood up in his stirrups and brought his hand to his holster. He saw a figure standing in a thicket and shot at it with his .38. He heard another store-bought cartridge pop and felt lead whizzing by his head, taking off his hat, which flew a good fifteen yards and landed in a hollow. (The next day Odilon, his other boy, went there and found it. It was all full of holes.) Rodolfo took two more shots with the .38 and the figure ran off into the thicket and vanished in the darkness. Then he opened the gate with his arm and head bleeding, got to his house, called Nathan, and they went to town. Blood was running into his eyes and at times he could hardly see.

When he got dizzy and swayed in the saddle, Nathan would say, "Careful, Father, you're going to fall."

He would right himself and think, I can't faint, or I'll die here on the road with my mouth full of dirt.

There was no doctor in the town, only a pharmacist, whom they wakened. Rodolfo told him that they had been hunting and Nathan's shotgun went off and the lead hit him. The pharmacist made him lie down and gave him some medicine so he wouldn't faint. Then he cleaned and disinfected the wounds, put some salve on them, and wrapped Rodolfo's arm and head in gauze. And he said that Rodolfo should go to the city to look up a doctor and get an X ray to make sure there was no more lead in his arm or his scalp. He told Rodolfo he had been lucky not to get killed. But Rodolfo didn't go to the city. He thought he didn't need to because, after he took the medicine, went home, ate and slept a bit, the sensation of fainting disappeared. His arm swelled up and hurt for a few days; then it stopped hurting and healed. And Rodolfo thought about things. He saw that the clouds, covering the moon at the moment he reached the gate, had made the person's aim bad. But even so, he hadn't died because, he said, "Whoever it was doesn't understand hunting."

If he did, he wouldn't shoot at a man with those store-bought cartridges. "Worthless cartridges, hardly any lead in them," he reasoned. "And Sinésio Silva never goes hunting."

He didn't go to see Janice anymore. He didn't forget her, but he didn't go to her house again. And he didn't even stop in the bars for a drink. "If I drink, I might end up saying something I shouldn't," he said to himself. He just did his work and began going out only in the daytime, being careful to vary his route and always taking along Nathan or Odilon. They went armed and rode about ten yards from each other.

"That way he can't get me," he said, watching the thickets and trees along the roads.

Four months after he was shot, he prepared some very heavy cartridges with lots of lead and plenty of gunpowder. He waited for the Feast of the Rosary in the town, knowing Sinésio Silva liked parties. Rodolfo chose a place along the way where there were some trees and lay in wait for him. The feast lasted three days, and on the first night Sinésio didn't pass by. The second night he appeared. He was alone, going in the direction of Janice's house. Rodolfo recognized the horse. He propped the cartridge box against a tree trunk, let him go past, and then shot. Aimed for the middle of his back and shot. Sinésio Silva lurched forward and fell. The night was clear and Rodolfo could see easily when the shot hit him, lifting his shoulders and arms, making his head jerk up. The horse ran away and Sinésio stayed on the ground, quiet. Rodolfo waited awhile and, as nothing happened, came out and moved cautiously up to have a look. Sinésio continued motionless and Rodolfo turned him over, looked into his face, and so as to have no doubt, took his .38 out of his belt and shot him again in the forehead.

Janice went back to the city and Rodolfo started seeing her right away. People said a lot of things, but there were no witnesses and they couldn't prove anything against anyone. Rodolfo took Janice to live in a house on one of his ranches. He went to see her almost every day, always varying the route and never saying what time he was going to arrive or leave.

The waters also covered the Veridiana Ranch, where a beautiful girl had been born. Her name was Denise. When she was a little girl, coming home from town with her father, mother, and three brothers, she let her horse stray over and poke its muzzle into the trough where a herd of donkeys was eating corn. One of them bit Denise's horse and the animals started to trade kicks and bites. Denise fell off. Lying on her back on the ground, she could see their hooves and legs stamping around and above her. Still on her back, she tried to squirm away from the donkeys and the horse but couldn't. Then she felt two hands pulling her out. They were her father's.

"You let the horse go in among the burros when they're eating?" he cried. "They might have killed you!"

Without her realizing it, one of the animals had stepped on her arm, hurting it and leaving a mark in the form of a half-moon. She never forgot that experience: lying on the ground, trying to get out from under the legs, bellies, and feet of the animals trampling so close to her. Sometimes she even dreamed she was escaping from some danger, going too slowly, desperate because her father's hands didn't come to pull her away.

The waters covered this ranch where Denise was born and the neighboring ranches of Sr. Mauro and Sr. Cosme Abraham. Both of them had claimed possession of a particular piece of land along the river, and Mauro won the case. Twenty years later he concluded that the judge's decision had been one-sided and he gave the land back.

Cosme Abraham was old, sick, and bedridden, but nevertheless he got up, went to Mauro's house, and kissed the doorsill, saying, "Here lives a blessed man."

The little cemetery containing the grave of Eugênio's mother was also covered by the waters. Eugênio was the youngest of eight children, and from age ten to twelve he worked for an uncle named Bernardo. He hauled firewood to the city on donkeyback. He would drive the donkeys along, walking exactly twenty-six kilometers every day. He went barefoot, often crossing long stretches where the ground was covered with sharp rocks. At night he complained of pains in his legs. His mother would put the kettle on the stove and fix him a footbath. His father and older brothers would pass through the kitchen, see him sitting on the stool, and watch his mother bending over to bathe his feet and legs with hot water.

"What's this nonsense, Adelaide?" his father would ask.

"Eugênio's feet hurt," she explained.

"Aw, his feet hurt! He's a sissy!" the brothers would say. And they would add, "Mother, you'll end up spoiling that boy."

His uncle paid very little, so he went with two other brothers to work for a reforesting company located beyond a town called Santa Rita. The place was remote and he, his brothers, and sixteen other men had to travel three days in a truck bed to reach it. Although it was distant, the job was easy and paid well. All they had to do was mix earth, sand, and manure to fill up small plastic sacks, then put in the seeds. They also had to water the beds where the seedlings had been started and cover them with straw. When it was time to plant them, you had to remember to poke a hole in the little sacks. They slept in rough wooden barracks with spaces between the boards, and on foggy mornings, leeches would climb up the walls and bedframes. They were dark-colored leeches, bigger than your fingers. It made Eugênio nauseous to think they could climb up and latch on to his arms and legs.

One of the men explained that salt would get rid of them, but the cook said, "I haven't got salt to waste on such foolishness."

At night Eugênio would make plans to steal some salt from the kitchen the next day and sprinkle it around his bed. He would make plans but wouldn't move from the middle of the mattress. He was afraid to get near the edges and wake up the next day covered with leeches sucking his blood. The roofs had no ceiling, and bats and mosquitoes came into the barracks as well. All night long you could hear the drone of the mosquitoes and see the bats flying overhead, shadows that passed quickly and silently between the beds. Eugênio battled to stay awake, to keep away from the edges of the mattress, and to stay completely covered with the sheet, because that way the bats and mosquitoes could not get at him. When he felt sleep overpowering him, he would cover his head with the filthy cloth. He would wrap himself up, face and all, not caring if he almost suffocated. While they were working with the seedlings, the other men remarked about the spots the cook had on his arms, face, and neck. They said they were caused by leprosy, that they were eating food prepared by a leper and at any time a piece of finger could fall into the beans or rice. Eugênio, at lunch and supper, looked carefully at his plate, and every day he eyed the cook's hands to see if he continued to have ten fingers.

Then one day a man came down with fever and they said, "It's malaria."

The man burned with fever, drenched in sweat.

"He won't make it," the others commented.

And indeed he died. He died at night, and the next morning they found him stiffened, with his mouth and eyes open. They took him up to a cemetery on top of a hill to bury him. There was no road so they loaded the coffin on an ox cart.

Eugênio climbed up on the cart while the others

walked, drinking and talking. He had to brace himself tight because of the bumps, and he watched as the coffin, made of rough boards and hammered together by drunken men, slid back and forth and banged apart. The dead man's legs came out and they stopped the ox cart. They tied a rope around the coffin to hold the legs in and went on. It was getting dark. They had all drunk so much they miscalculated the size of the grave. When they discovered that they had dug it too short, they didn't make it longer. They only made it a little deeper, stuck the coffin in any old which way, and covered it with dirt. Eugênio would listen to the humming of the mosquitoes at night and think that they were the same ones that had bitten the dead man. They would bite him and he, too, would catch the disease, die, and be buried on that hilltop with his legs tied into the coffin by a rope. It was then he decided that he wasn't staying there any longer, he was going home.

"Going home to Mama?" his brothers wanted to know.

They called him a sissy. He didn't care; he went back alone. His father immediately asked why he didn't want to keep on working there and he answered, "I didn't like it."

"Your brothers did but you didn't?" and turning to his wife: "Didn't I say that boy would turn out good for nothing?"

Eugênio now knew what his labor was worth and didn't accept his uncle's job back. He began to sharecrop on nearby farms and to buy and sell things. When his brothers came home and told him how much he would be earning if he had stayed where they were, he paid no attention. One day after he was married, an opportunity arose for him to sell everything he had and buy a piece of land.

His father commented, "What would you do with that land? Raise lizards?"

He said it was very poor land and enumerated the people who had owned it, all of whom had gone broke. Eugênio thought about it and spoke to his mother.

"Father says that if I buy it, I'll go broke, too, because Breno, Devair, and Hector all bought that land and lost money on it."

"Breno only wanted to fish and hunt partridges," his mother answered. "He never thought of anything else, just fishing and hunting."

Devair had built a sugar mill and a still to produce rum, though there was no sugarcane on the land.

"He's somebody who doesn't know what's good for him."

Hector was no businessman. "He buys pigs at a price, fattens them, and sells them for less than he paid." Then she told her son, "You're a hard worker and you know how to take care of what's yours. Go and have a look at the land. See what you can make of it."

He went, saw that the land was broad and fertile. There was a lot of underbrush and scrub trees, but the land itself was good. It had only been poorly cared for. So he bought it, cut down the brush, cleaned out the weeds. At once good grass began to spring up. He dismantled and sold the sugar mill and distillery Devair had built, though everyone said he was crazy.

"How will you support your family? Raising lizards?" his father asked.

"No, Father, I'm not going to raise lizards, I'm going to raise cattle."

With the money from the sugar mill and the distillery he bought some cows, and they were the beginning of everything he earned from then on. He never sold the land. He ended up with far more than his father and brothers, and when his mother died and was buried in the little cemetery near where they lived, he who from the age of twelve wouldn't set foot in a cemetery lost his fear of them. On All Souls' Day and Christmas he would take flowers and pray over his mother's grave.

But the waters came and covered the cemetery. They covered the house where Marcelino lived, a man who only thought of making money. He and his sons had few friends and were in the habit of going out at night to hunt. Once a young man passing through became sweethearts with one of the daughters, and when he left without asking her to marry him, she drank poison and died. The family, who had few friends, became even more inhospitable toward strangers and didn't let anyone set foot on their land. People said the daughter's death was just an excuse. They didn't like anyone coming around because they had lots of things hidden on their ranch. It was rumored that they went to the interior, stole livestock, and sold it to the boatmen.

"You can't trust them," people said.

One day the horse of a man called Stephen disappeared and he went looking for it. They said it might have strayed onto Marcelino's pastures and Stephen went to the ranch house and asked permission to look.

"Your horse hasn't been around here," said Marcelino. Stephen wasn't satisfied and insisted. Marcelino asked, "Don't you trust us?" They had this conversation outside the house. Marcelino's three sons were hanging around nearby, in silence.

"No, that's not it," answered Stephen. "But people said my horse might have come this way."

"Well, people say a lot of things, but I'm saying that it isn't on my land. What more do you want?"

Stephen went away and later found his horse loose on the road. One of its legs was hamstrung, and the strong, steady gait it had had was spoiled. Stephen thought Marcelino's people had crippled the animal out of malice. So when some cows belonging to a cousin of his disappeared, he started going out early to a hill where, from behind a tree, he watched Marcelino and his sons doing business with the boatmen. They sold produce and horses, cattle and pack burros. They would make ramps of boards between the riverbank and the sides of the boats in order to load the animals. Stephen wanted to see if they would load his cousin's cows. Marcelino's people saw that they were being watched and one of the sons, named Edésio, went over and swore at Stephen. The two argued and Stephen kicked the son, who dodged away and pulled out a knife. He stabbed Stephen in the belly. Then he ran off, leaving the other with his belly ripped open, trying to hold his intestines in with his hands. Nobody helped him. No one from Marcelino's family came over to see what had happened and he ended up dying. He died on the hilltop, under the tree. Afterward people were afraid to pass by there at night. They said that the tree was haunted and that, at midnight, whoever went by and looked in that direction would see a ghost leaning against the trunk and groaning. And if you asked, "What do you want, soul of

God?" it would answer, "I want the help that no one gave me."

Stephen's brothers and cousins were revolted, outraged. They couldn't believe such a thing had happened.

"It can't be," they said. "The father of a family just can't be killed like that, as if he were a pig."

The police went looking for Edésio but didn't find him. One day Dalmo, Stephen's cousin, saw Edésio on the road, came up, and shot him dead. The law officer of the town, afraid that a feud between the families would bring more deaths, gave his sergeant orders to find Dalmo no matter what and arrest him. The sergeant and four more soldiers tracked him down and found him in the house of one of Stephen's brothers. But they couldn't get close; the men in the house were armed and shooting. The sergeant yelled that he was following orders, he didn't want to kill anyone, just to arrest the criminal. It was no good, they didn't let him get near. He warned them that he would take Dalmo no matter what.

"I have my orders," he shouted.

They surrounded the house and began to shoot. Those inside shot back. All sorts of people came up, attracted by the gunfire. They took cover behind trees or stretched on the ground at a distance to watch.

The sergeant prepared a bottle full of kerosene to throw inside the house and see if he could set it on fire, but the people behind the trees said to him. "You're not going to roast the women and children, are you, Sergeant?"

So then he yelled in to Dalmo, "If you want to resist arrest, that's your problem, but send the women and children out."

Soon the door opened and six children and three women came out. The women had to drag the oldest boy after them; he was crying, wanting to go back inside the house. The sergeant tried to talk with the women but they went quickly off into the trees. However, he talked with the boy and learned that inside the house were Dalmo and two of Stephen's brothers. He made a few attempts to use the bottleful of kerosene but didn't manage to get close enough to throw it. The day passed. Even from far away people could hear the shots and see what was happening. Everybody there liked Dalmo and Stephen and disliked Marcelino and his sons. The sergeant saw the hordes of people crouched behind the trees and hillocks and became worried.

He sent for Sr. Petrónio, Dalmo's father, and said, "He killed a man, and we have to set things right before the law."

"Yes, but you didn't arrest the man who murdered Stephen," commented Petrónio.

"That wasn't our fault. He disappeared and your son was the first to find him, and he killed him. Now Dalmo has to be taken in," the sergeant reasoned.

Petrónio wasn't convinced, and the sergeant called over Dona Celeste, Dalmo's mother. He promised that nothing would happen to her son if he gave himself up. He gave his word of honor that he would only take Dalmo, the other two could go free. He spoke in a loud voice so that everyone could hear and be witnesses. Dona Celeste talked to her husband, and they went inside the house together and came back out with Dalmo. The soldiers took him prisoner. On the day of the trial the whole family came to town and sat in the courtroom until the very end. He was condemned to seven years and the family claimed that the defense lawyer had been bought off by Marcelino's people.

Besides the lands and houses of these people, the waters also covered the house where Elisa and her brother, Durval, lived. They were two children, she five years old and he just a few months under three. They always had their baths out in the yard. Elisa would stand in a basin while her mother threw water over her head with a dipper and lathered her arms, back, neck; cleaned her ears. The children would talk constantly, only stopping when their faces were being washed. Every afternoon Elisa and her brother had their baths in the yard. She always went first, then her brother. When her bath was finished, Elisa would climb up on a bench and begin drying herself while her mother changed the water and called Durval. He wouldn't stay quiet. Their mother had to hold him by the arm so he wouldn't sit down in the basin or grab the dipper, the sponge, the soap. He would splash around, complaining that the sponge was scratching, the soap was hurting his eyes, or the water was too hot or too cold.

He would say, "Stop, Mother!"

The mother, after drying him, would dress him with his shirt buttoned in the back so he wouldn't undo it and go around bare-chested. One day, as she was buttoning the boy's shirt, she noticed that her daughter was scratching her heel very hard.

"Let's see that heel," she said. And she discovered that Elisa had a sand flea in her foot. She went into the house, got a needle, put its point into a flame to disinfect it, bent over, and began to take out the parasite. She made a small opening all around the black point, around the eye of the creature. She made the hole carefully so the parasite would come out whole, without breaking apart.

"It doesn't hurt at all," she was saying. "It'll come out all in one piece."

Elisa let her mother prick her foot, though she was a little scared. Durval pushed between the two of them to look, interested and curious. He examined his own heels to see if he might have a sand flea, too. When their mother was finished, she showed them the tiny round object on the point of the needle.

"See there?" she said. "It came out all in one piece."

She destroyed the sand flea by burning it in a match flame, put methiolate on Elisa's foot, and then had to attend to Durval, who wanted her to look at his feet.

She checked them carefully, kissed them, and said, "Not a single one."

Then she made them put their shoes on. After their bath she would go in to get supper, and the children waited on the veranda for their father to come home from work. Their mother always warned them not to go beyond the gate. Some drivers had the habit of coming down the street very fast, and she was scared the children would go out on the sidewalk and be hit by a car. Elisa's father was named Heleno. He was a barber and he had an *azulão*, a jaybird that sang beautifully. Sometimes, when he went out in the morning, he would cover the cage with a cloth and take the bird to the barbershop. When he left it home, he would hang the cage on the porch, and when he got back in the evening, he would put it back onto a nail on the wall of the corridor. One day when he came home from the barbershop, the bird was entirely featherless. There wasn't a single feather on its body, just on its head. It sat on the bottom of the cage looking skinny, ugly, bony. Its head seemed too big. It looked like a chicken about to be put in the pan. Heleno became quite worried, and he and his wife discussed the matter a long time, trying to imagine who could have done such a thing. They reached the conclusion that it might have been a neighbor or someone who passed by the house every day and was jealous because the bird sang so well. The person could have come onto the porch and left the bird in its terrible state. The woman and the children were almost always indoors and the person, not seeing anyone, had calmly done the mischief. Heleno thought the bird would die. He heard that okra broth mixed with *ora pro nobis* leaves was a good medicine and he began to rub the bird's body with this mixture. He also put the bird in the tub when he bathed and gave it water to drink. He transferred the cage to his room to keep it out of drafts and continued the treatment faithfully. The bird's feathers grew in again, and it became as healthy as before.

One Sunday, many days later, he, his wife, and the two children were on the veranda. Elisa was playing with a puzzle and Durval with a hobbyhorse, when Elisa confessed, "It was me who plucked the jay."

"What? What did you do?" Heleno asked, surprised.

"I plucked the feathers off the little bird."

"You did that, daughter?"

"Yes, Father."

"And why did you do that?"

"No reason," she answered.

She had done it because she wanted to see what the

bird looked like without its feathers. She had climbed up on a chair, stuck her hand in the cage, grabbed the bird, and pulled off all its blue-green feathers, one by one.

"Didn't you feel sorry for the little bird, daughter?" her mother asked.

"No," she answered.

"It hurts him when you pull off his feathers. Without them he can't fly, and he gets cold. But even so, you didn't feel sorry for him?" Heleno wanted to know.

"No. He didn't die," Elisa said, without looking up from her puzzle.

Two other men worked in the barbershop with Heleno. They were called Ivanir and Juarez. Ivanir played the banjo and his wife, Josiana, couldn't stand to hear him play it when she was pregnant. He liked to practice when night fell, after they had eaten supper. He would sit in front of the window of the living room and pick at the banjo. Josiana, from the very beginning of her pregnancy, was irritated by this. She was irritated at his banjo playing and also by other things, like Sr. Nero, from whom she always bought fish. She couldn't stand to see the stump of his amputated leg moving when he stretched up to put the fish onto the scales for his customers. The summer heat made her angry, too. She would perspire and curse the weather. She kept all the windows of the house open, not permitting a single one to be shut. Not even those of the bedroom. She slept all night with them open.

Juarez, the other barber, always talked about soccer as he shaved his customers and trimmed their hair. He was the founder of a team called the Advancers. He was also its director and took care of the uniforms as well. Juarez always contributed most toward the purchase of new shirts and balls. At one time he had been a good player, but his physical endurance gradually diminished and he couldn't run fast enough to follow long passes. Still he insisted on playing on the team, which in the end hurt their average. Since everybody recognized his love and dedication to the Advancers and didn't want to offend him, his teammates themselves designed a plan to make him quit. They began to pass all the balls to him, to place him in frontal offensives, side attacks.

During training and games all you heard was, "Get this one, Juarez!"

"Go for it, Juarez!"

"It's yours, Juarez."

When it rained and the field was wet, the players would comment, "With this mud in the penalty zone, you're the only one who can get through, Juarez."

And they fed Juarez the ball so much that when time-outs came he could hardly stand up. After a while he began to realize that he wasn't as good as he used to be. He started asking to be replaced in the middle of the game, then playing only occasionally. Finally he only discussed soccer, though he continued to finance and encourage the Advancers.

In the house next door to the barbershop lived Dona Laísa, a teacher at the local school who was a great favorite with her students. When she got married, the church was all decorated with white flowers and her students filled the pews on the right and on the left sides. She came in on her father's arm, smiling and very happy. But the children wouldn't be quiet. They made all kinds of noise, traded places, talked too loud. Laísa interrupted her entrance and, with the groom and attendants waiting at the altar, straightened things out. Right there in the church, she called for order, told the children to be quiet. She had the girls sit on one side and the boys on the other. And she warned, "Now then. I don't want any of you talking or changing places."

She was used to maintaining discipline in the classroom and didn't care for such disorderly behavior. After settling the children, she took her father's arm again and went happily down the aisle to meet her groom.

The house on the other side of the barbershop once belonged to a man called Zé Quincas. He was the father of eight, and he had a very high voice, strange for a man. He owned a car and would hire out to drive people places. One night, coming home from a trip, he ran into a truck. No one got hurt, but even so he was already beginning to tire of his work.

He said in his high, strident voice, "I don't want anything more to do with this heap."

And sure enough, he had the car fixed and sold it. He used the money to make a down payment on a piece of land that he had been wanting to buy for a long time. The land had an orchard and very good water running through the middle of the property.

Zé Quincas would say, "I've got the best water in the world. I can irrigate any part of my land I want."

The water flowed in where the ground was higher and descended in a small stream. Before flowing into the river it formed a marsh that Zé Quincas promised to drain and build tanks to raise fish. His wife had the house and eight children to take care of and couldn't be bothered with her husband's business, but nevertheless she gave him advice, which he ignored.

"I'm going to buy a piece of land and plant beans," he used to say when he owned the car.

So he did what he promised: he planted beans and left his oldest children to take care of the plot while he waited for harvest time. They would go to the bean plot every day to weed and clean it. Zé Quincas went out to do business, because he had to support his family. He bought a load of salt and manioc flour in a place many hours' journey away. He rented a truck and went along with the driver to pick up the load. They arrived as it was getting dark and the owner, who knew who he was, let them take the merchandise and pay later. Zé Quincas never went back and the owner came looking for him. The man discovered where he lived, but only found the house and the wife and eight children frightened and unable to give him any information about his whereabouts. Later Zé Quincas appeared driving a station wagon. He acquired other merchandise and didn't pay for it or the station wagon either. And lots of people came looking for him, to collect their money.

One day Zé Quincas's mother-in-law died, leaving a farm and two houses in the town. She had been a widow and there were six children. Right away Zé Quincas wanted to receive his wife's share of the inheritance. The lawyer responsible for the inventory explained to him that it would take some time to settle the estate. Zé Quincas thought it was entirely too slow and began to say they were making the inheritance into a legal muddle.

"Somebody's holding this business up," he would say in his squeaky voice.

He went around saying that they were delaying the division of property in order to benefit his brothers-in-law.

"There's bribe money changing hands."

He created a lot of bad feeling, talking about documents that his wife's relatives must be passing back and forth secretly.

"But it makes no difference, I still want my part," he commented so everyone could hear him.

His brothers-in-law had no sympathy for him whatsoever. They missed their mother, whose death had been a shock. Seeing Zé Quincas wanting to get his hands on everything, making demands to have his part right away, they explained that first it was necessary to sell the farm and the houses. The oldest couldn't tolerate Zé Quincas's attitude. One day he overheard Zé Quincas say that the judge needed to know a few things "to straighten out this disgrace." The brother-in-law grabbed him by the collar and said, "We'll straighten it out right now."

He dragged him to the courthouse, promising as they went through the streets to blow his head off with a gun at any minute. He called him a son of a bitch and warned him, "You'd better respect my mother's memory."

They went into the courthouse, the brother-in-law dragging him by the collar. Zé Quincas was pale, murmuring, "You're awfully nervous."

The judge received them out of consideration to the brother-in-law and explained to Zé Quincas the time limits and legal formalities that were involved in settling an estate. After that Zé Quincas waited to receive his share of the inheritance without complaining in public. But at home he complained to his wife and accused his brothers-in-law of cheating.

Beyond this street where the barbershop was and where Laísa the teacher and Zé Quincas lived, there was a small square that was called Intendente Fernando Pimenta Square. There resided a woman called Dulcinea. She did embroidery for a living, and five years after she was widowed married Adolfo, manager of the Hotel Bandeirantes, a quiet-living man who kept the hotel very clean and ran it efficiently. Dulcinea raised chickens in her backyard, where you could see their nests inside baskets that had been whitewashed, "to keep the fleas down," she explained.

She had been married to a man who worked in the drugstore, but they hadn't had children. Her husband was known as Pedro Pavio and had died one night during a fishing expedition with some friends. They hooked an enormous fish, and the boat was rocked hard. Pedro Pavio lost his balance and fell into the water. He was only found three days later, already much chewed by the fish.

Dulcinea and Adolfo met when he went to ask her if she could embroider the name of the hotel on the bed linens, towels, and tablecloths. At that time he hadn't dated anyone or gone after women for some time. He was traumatized by the death of a girl named Brigit, whom he had met in the red-light zone during a party with some friends. They had met at a table and had a drink. Then they went up to her room. He liked the way she made love and began to visit her often. Soon they were seeing each other almost every day. Adolfo would wait for her to finish attending the other men and then go into her room. He would lie down, and they would make love and converse calmly. Brigit began to be fond of him and to have illusions that he would take her to live with him. He went along with her insinuations and let her make plans. But when Brigit started showing up at the hotel and crying when he left her room, Adolfo got worried. One day he had a frank conversation with her. He invented a story: he was engaged to the daughter of a rancher and was going to be married. He didn't like the girl and had been putting off the marriage, but he couldn't do it any longer. They had known each other since childhood, the families were friends, and everyone—parents, relatives, mutual friends—was pressuring him. There was no way to put it off any longer. So he and Brigit would have to stop meeting. When he told her this, she showed no reaction, just looked apathetically at the bed, but when he got dressed to leave, she asked him a favor: that they could meet one last time, in two days.

"The day after tomorrow I'll be twenty-three," she said.

So it would be sort of a going-away party and a birthday celebration in one. Adolfo agreed. When he went to meet her, he brought her a new jacket, since he had noticed that hers was practically threadbare. Brigit was wearing a new dress. They went into the bedroom, had a drink, talked, and at one point she went into the bathroom. When she came back, she turned off the light, they embraced and began to make love. During their lovemaking, in the dark, she didn't speak. She only writhed about a lot, at times moaning and stiffening her muscles. When it was over, he reached out and turned on the light. A white foam was running out of her mouth: she was dying. She had drunk soda pop mixed with ant poison when she went to the bathroom, and her movements had been convulsions rather than movements of pleasure. She had been dying while they made love.

This experience left him much traumatized. He lost all desire for women. The mere thought of being with them, making love to them, caused him an awful sensation of nausea and repulsion. One of his friends knew what had happened and, at times, invited him to come along to the whorehouses.

"I can't," he would say.

The friend would insist and he would explain, "I just can't do it."

His friend would keep on insisting, telling him, "Forget that woman. She's dead and buried." When he was drunk, he would add, "She doesn't exist. Not even her ashes exist anymore."

It was no use, Adolfo couldn't forget Brigit's movements underneath him as she was dying, consuming herself in pain while he felt pleasure.

"She took the poison because of me," he said. "The two of us making love and her dying."

The thought left his body as cold as ice. And when he and his friend went drinking, and the friend insisted he forget about Brigit, the memory would grow intolerable and he would walk off down the street. It was as if one day that memory would suffocate him.

When he went to speak to Dulcinea about embroidering the bed linens and towels, he was thirty years old, and she was thirty-five. They talked about the work she was to do and about other things. She seemed very sincere and understanding and they talked for over two hours. The next evening he went back and they talked again, for even longer. And he told her what had happened. It was the first time that he had spoken about Brigit with a woman. She listened attentively. The next day he talked about Brigit again, and once more Dulcinea listened. They became friends. Then they started dating, and they grew so close that one day they embraced, kissed, and made love without Adolfo feeling any nausea or repulsion. After that they got married.

In this square also lived Marcílio, who had a car for hire and knew all the roads, detours, and byways of the region. When his father turned eighty, Marcílio convinced him to sell his little ranch and move into town.

"You can come and live with us," he said.

His wife and brothers were against the idea. They thought it wasn't right to tear the old man away from the surroundings where he had worked his whole life. Where he had been born, married, watched his children grow up and make their own way. Where he had grown old, lost his wife.

"Father leave his ranch?" the brothers said. "He'd never adjust! He'd die."

"But he can't go on living the way he is, all alone," argued Marcílio. "Suppose he gets sick all of a sudden. Who would help him?"

Although his brothers and wife were against it, he convinced his father to sell the ranch and move to town. As he had promised, Marcílio set up a stall for him in the marketplace, near the river, where he could sell medicinal herbs and roots and give advice on their use. The old man had always enjoyed doing this. He got along very well. Everyone, including Marcílio, was surprised with his quick adjustment. In a short time he became well known and people came from miles away to ask him questions and order his medicines. Marcílio had to take him out looking for roots, herbs, and animals. The father made friends with the boatmen and asked them to bring him products that he couldn't find in those parts. His room in Marcílio's house soon became a storage place for leaves, seeds, dry branches, grains, fruits, glass jars full of alcohol in which he pickled snakes, caterpillars, pieces of wood. The plasters he prepared became famous for curing any sort of noxious animal bite.

"He can even cure the sting of brown scorpions," people declared.

When they closed the floodgates of the dam and the waters began to rise, he was eighty-six years old and making plans to buy some plots of ground on the outskirts of the town where he could plant the species hardest to find.

Marcílio's neighbor was Vicêncio, a great admirer of singing canaries. Behind his house was a veranda where he hung his cages. There were many of them, each with its canary. They were in rows, very close to each other, and there were pieces of board between them so that the birds wouldn't see each other. In the afternoon, he and his friends would sit on the veranda and listen to the bird song. They sat in silence, measuring the length of the trills, comparing the melodies, appreciating. Every so often someone would speak, remembering a famous canary they had known. Vicêncio had had the best one of all. It was called Watch Eye, because one of its pupils turned white one day, and soon it went blind in that eye. It started singing less, and there were fewer notes in its warble. Soon the other pupil went white, too. The bird couldn't see out of either eye and stopped singing altogether. But it knew its way around the cage and learned to eat and drink without assistance. It would jump off the perch and walk along the sides of the cage to the corner where the water and birdseed were in order to eat and drink. Sometime later it started singing again and surpassed all the others. Its way of singing was like that of canaries from Bahia. When Watch Eye died, a friend of Vicêncio's friends who had once photographed the bird had the photo enlarged and framed so Vicêncio could hang it on the wall of the veranda.

"Watch Eye used to pick on the other birds," the men would recall.

And when Vicêncio looked at the picture he would comment, "Look there, he was doing one of his long trills. See the way he was opening his beak?"

In the street that gave onto the square was a spiritist center. The sessions were at night and the people went in barefoot. Everyone had to leave his shoes, boots, sandals, or thongs outside near the door. Inside, during the sessions, the medium commanded the people to lift their hands upward and pray as he received messages from the spirits. The congregation was supposed to keep their eyes closed. Individuals who seemed more charged with spirits were led up in front of the medium by his helpers. He would touch their heads and wave his hands in front of their eyes, and the spirits would come out of them. Occasionally people fell to the floor and needed to be lifted up and supported until they stopped their contortions and went back to normal. The medium did operations, too. The person desiring surgery was supposed to go home, concentrate on the sickness that was tormenting him, and at a time determined by the spirit, lie down in bed. Then he would feel the sickness leaving his body. Afterward he should drink several glasses of water, sleep until the next day, and would be ready to get up, entirely cured. Some husbands took their wives but didn't go into the center; they would sit in a bar and drink while the session was on, waiting for the wives to come out.

There were other houses on that street. There was one painted pink where Clélio lived with his wife, Laurita, and three children, ages four, two, and one. Clélio had always been very impatient when the children cried, and if one of them began to cry at night, he would put the child inside a large basket in the living room so as not to hear the screaming.

There was also Tarcísio's house. It was well built, set back from the street. It had grass in the front, white walls, and blue doors and window frames. Tarcísio took more than two years to build it, and he began when he asked for Adalgisa's hand in marriage. He worked in an accounting office and built the house little by little with only a stonemason and the stonemason's helper. Tarcísio himself would give a hand on Saturday afternoons, Sundays, and holidays. At that time the priest was raising funds to finish the church and he asked the faithful to donate money and construction materials. The priest began to notice that Tarcísio never donated anything. Neither money nor material.

Once, greeting Tarcísio and his fiancée after Mass, the priest asked, "Why don't you contribute some of the bricks and cement from your building project to our work at the church, my son?"

"Times are hard, Father, and I can hardly manage to buy what I need for my house."

The priest didn't like this answer, and he commented to Adalgisa's mother that she should orient her daughter better, for the girl was about to become the wife of a young man who wasn't too commendable. An egotistical young man. The mother spoke with Adalgisa and she told Tarcísio. He complained to the priest, who, besides confirming what he had said, called Tarcísio a lost sheep to boot. And he added, "This selfishness will get you nowhere. Your house will never be a sure refuge for you and your family."

The true refuge would always be the house of God. "And it has priority over everything."

"I'm only minding my own business, Father," Tarcísio said in self-justification.

"That's just the attitude that will be your undoing," the priest told him. To Adalgisa he said, "Think carefully, daughter, about the person you are joining yourself to for eternity."

Tarcísio got very angry and stalked out of the church grumbling to his fiancée, "Whoever heard of such a thing? I'm making an effort to build our future, the security of our family, and he calls me selfish. A lost sheep!"

Adalgisa's mother insisted that he donate bricks and cement to the church.

"I can't," Tarcísio said. "I don't have enough money."

So when a very hard rain made part of the sacristy wall fall down, he commented to the mother-in-law, "See that?

It's God's punishment. That priest is wrong to say such things about me."

But still the mother-in-law never forgave him for the misunderstanding, and whenever any difficulty or privation arose, she always asked God to pardon her for not managing to get her daughter away from that man. But it was all covered up by the waters. Not only the houses, the streets, the church, but also a place known as Indian Hollow, which had this name because a long time ago a village of Caiapós Indians had existed there. The ranchers and lots of men from the town got together and surrounded it, to put an end to the stealing and livestock rustling that was happening in the region. They surrounded the village and after only a few shots they took all the Indians prisoner. The Indians had no firearms, and furthermore, a priest had gone with the ranchers to give extreme unction to those who might be wounded or dying. When the Indians saw the priest, they gave themselves up without a fight. They respected priests, and seeing his frock, they stopped fighting. The ranchers tied them all up. Not the women, but all the male Indians older than twelve or thirteen were tied up and taken to a place on the riverbank. The ranchers and townsmen spent the night arguing and trying to figure out what to do with them. They decided that if they were really going to stop the robberies and attacks in the region, the best thing was to finish the Indians off. So they killed them one by one. The priest interfered, trying to save the younger ones, insisting that they shouldn't kill them, but it was no use.

"At least spare these," he pleaded. "They're very young, they're still children."

But it was no use. They shot every last one, all with their muskets. People said there had been more than two hundred Indians.

Right beside Indian Hollow was situated the land belonging to Galeno, a man over six feet tall, father of nine. Before he got married at age twenty, he had left home to work in a crystal mine. There was no water there, and he and his companions would work from sunup to sundown breaking rocks and only took baths on Saturdays, when the owner of the mine took them to the river in his pickup truck. Afterward he would loan them horses so they could go to parties. It was common for them to travel great distances to have some fun. They were strong men, and together they got into the habit of riding into small, poor towns and causing an uproar. They would put out the lanterns, fire shots into the air, shout at the musicians, and force the girls to dance with them. Sometimes people would be frightened by their noisy arrival and start to run. The men would shoot into the air and command everybody to stay where they were. That was worse. The people would escape through the windows or hide under their beds. The men thought it was funny and laughed all the harder. One day they went to a place called Vista das Palmas, where the Petrobras oil company was drilling a well and employed a great many workers. It was forty-five miles away and they went in the pickup truck belonging to the man who owned the crystal mine. The party was in a village square that had been fenced off so that only those who bought tickets could get in. There were raffles, dancing, booths with things for sale. Some soldiers were on guard to keep out anyone who was armed. The Petrobras men went around in black and yellow jeeps, and their foreman, a Negro called Guaraci, stayed close to the soldiers, helping to maintain order. Galeno and his companions left their guns in the pickup and went in. He and some of the others went to dance. Galeno saw a good-looking girl and asked her to dance.

"I'm already taken," she said. "I only dance with my fiancé."

Galeno didn't like that, and when they stopped the music and began auctioning off roast chickens to help with the expenses of the party, he bought the biggest, most expensive one. He received a red rose, which he immediately presented to the engaged girl, who was thus obliged to dance with him. That was the rule. He gave her the rose in front of everyone, and they began to dance. Right away Galeno started to hug her tightly and wouldn't let her sit down. The fiancé worked for Petrobras, as did his two brothers who were at the party. The fiancé walked onto the dance floor and pulled the girl by the arm. Galeno hit him in the chest and knocked him down. The brothers surrounded Galeno but didn't actually attack him. They could easily see how strong Galeno and his companions were, and they were afraid. They took the young man who was engaged outside and the girl went after them, crying. Galeno stayed inside looking at the other girls, choosing somebody else to dance with. Later one of his friends, Eloi by name, who had driven the pickup, called him over.

"The Petrobras guys are arming themselves," he said.

He pointed out Guaraci, the security chief, who was giving the men knives. He was behind a booth, in the dark, and the blades glinted when the men took them and hid the knives under their shirts.

"Let's get out of here," said the friend. "Let's go to the pickup and get our guns."

As the two of them were going out Eloi decided to warn the others.

"Give me the keys to the truck," said Galeno. "I'll go on ahead."

Eloi gave him the keys and went to call the others while Galeno went on. Before he could walk ten yards the lights went out. Everything was completely dark and some of the people started to shout, "That man's leaving!"

"Surround him!"

"Don't let him get away!"

Hearing that, Galeno said to himself, If they catch me, I'm in big trouble. So he started to run. Figures appeared in front of him and he changed direction. More figures appeared and he swerved again. Everywhere shadows jumped out, getting close, trying to surround him.

He ran, avoiding them, and voices shouted, "Don't let him escape!"

Everything was dark but he could see the glint of the knives in the hands of the figures. He fled in a zigzag, trying to get away from the square, until he realized he was surrounded. He fought his way out with blows and kicks and felt something cut his left shoulder. Bending over as he lunged out with his arm, he struck the figure that had knifed him. Galeno saw him close up, panting, still holding the knife. Grabbing on to the man's arm, he wrenched the knife away from him and stabbed him low in the belly. Then he pulled the knife upward, feeling that he was ripping the man apart, hearing him let out a hoarse groan. Galeno saw lights shining in the distance, near some houses, and tried to run toward them. Someone cut his right arm, and his chest and waist were scratched. He cut other people, too, and when he got away from the square, he heard shots behind him. He ran toward the houses, jumping over fences. A dog pursued him through several backyards until, barely able to breathe, he hid himself in a pigpen. He could hear voices very close by.

"We have to finish bleeding this man dry," one of the voices said.

When they went away, he came out of the pigpen and into a banana grove. He ran hard, tripping and falling into holes, bumping against tree trunks and leaves, slipping, but never slowing down until he reached a brook. He crossed it, went through some tall grass, and slowing to a walk, went as far as he could. Then he sat down under a tree, drowsed off, and woke up the next day with the sun in his face. His shoulder and the arm that had been cut hurt, and he was extremely thirsty. He started walking again, but soon heard voices approaching. There were some orange trees nearby, and he quickly climbed the biggest and leafiest of them. The voices came closer: two soldiers. They had followed his trail through the banana grove and the tall grass and were looking for him. They came right up to the orange tree and stopped to talk. Galeno's wounds began to bleed again, but he didn't move. He stayed there motionless, watching the blood run down his arm and drip onto the leaves and branches of the tree.

"He must be miles away by now," one of the soldiers said.

The soldier picked an orange off the tree and peeled it. Then they went away, and Galeno climbed down and hid himself in the forest. He stayed hidden until nightfall. He felt very weak but he knew that if he fell into the hands of the soldiers or the Petrobras workers, he was dead. When night came, he left his hiding place and began to walk, trying to keep away from the roads where the black and yellow jeeps might see him. As soon as the sun came up he hid himself again. He went on this way, lying low by day and moving by night. When it was dark, he walked, drank water from creeks, and ate whatever fruit he could find. And during the day he stayed hidden. He would spend hours without moving, quiet, listening to the wind and the songs of the birds. The wound in his shoulder got maggots in it. Galeno could see them crawling around, poking their heads out.

One day he was hidden near a river about six or seven yards wide when he heard voices and the sound of horses walking on the opposite bank. It was a man and his wife. The man was carrying a baby wrapped up in a blanket, and they were coming down the road through the forest. Galeno could hardly see them due to the trees, but he could hear them quite close to him. They stopped near a small footbridge and the man commented that the river had risen. The woman suggested that they cross on the footbridge with the child.

"Looks like it's rotten," the man said.

He handed the woman the child, dismounted, and went over to the bridge.

"Didn't I tell you?" he remarked, kicking it with his foot. "All rotten."

The water came right up to the trees, and even next to the footbridge the branches and leaves kept Galeno from seeing the couple or the horses properly. The man told the woman to ride across the water in front of him.

"You go first and see if we can ford."

The woman gave him back the baby and urged the horse ahead. It didn't want to go into the water and the man said, "Give her the spurs," and swore at the animal, "Damn no-good mare."

Spurred by the woman, the mare advanced into the water and grabbed a mouthful of grass. The woman slapped the animal with her riding crop and the mare went forward, swimming toward the bank where Galeno was. The bank was muddy and the mare had difficulty getting out. She would sink, her hooves sticking. The woman spurred and whipped her until the mare got up the bank very near Galeno's thicket. Then the man urged his horse into the water.

"Careful not to get Dimas wet," the woman said, referring to their son.

The man was carrying the child with his left hand and holding the reins with his right.

"We must be on Valderes's land," said the man. "He doesn't take care of anything."

A branch snagged the handle of a yellow bag that was tied behind the saddle. The handle broke and the bag fell into the water.

"Uh-oh! The bag with the bottle in it fell off."

"Don't let it get away," the woman said. "All Dimas's food is in it."

The man turned the horse around, forcing it to go after the bag.

"Don't let it get away," the woman repeated, and asked him, "Think you can get it?"

"Of course! I'm not dead yet," he answered, bending over on top of the saddle, almost lying down over the water. Soon he called, "Got it! Hell, now my clothes are all wet."

Holding the baby, the reins, and the bag, he guided the horse toward the bank. But the footing was too soft, and its hooves sank deep into the mud. The horse raised its head, sliding and struggling.

"Oh no, this saddle's coming loose!"

"What happened?" asked the woman.

"Damned girth strap broke!"

As the horse fought to get out of the water Galeno saw the saddle, with the man and child on top, go sliding backward over its rump.

"Watch out!" cried the woman. "Be careful with Dimas!" The man fell off along with the saddle and the woman screamed, "Don't let Dimas get wet!"

So as not to fall on top of the child, the man had to throw him to one side. The woman started to spur and whip her mare back down the bank into the water, but when the mare's hooves sank in the mud, she wouldn't go forward.

"Rinaldo!" the woman screamed to her husband. "Get Dimas!"

He couldn't answer, for he was struggling to keep above water and kick his feet out of the stirrups so he could be free of the saddle. Galeno saw the effort both of them made as the child, half-submerged, was carried downstream by the current.

"Get Dimas!" the woman screamed.

She jumped off the mare, sinking thigh-deep in the slippery clay. Then Galeno came out of his hiding place, slid down the bank onto the footbridge, and dived into the water. He felt weak, and sharp pains shot through his arm and shoulder. He jumped into the water, grabbed the child, and kept it above the surface as he went to meet the woman who was struggling over the clay bank. After a few strokes, his feet touched the sticky bottom, though he was already swallowing water and his lungs were bursting with weariness. But he managed to stay upright until the woman came and took the child from his hands. She went back to the water's edge, unwrapping him from the blanket, while Galeno, with water up to his chest, stood there too weak to move from where he was. The man finally got free of his stirrups.

"How's Dimas?" he yelled.

"He's all right," answered his wife.

The man got to the bank, pulling the saddle. The woman said, "Didn't I tell you it was better to cross over with him on the footbridge, didn't I tell you?"

"It's rotten! And how was I supposed to know the damn girth strap would break?"

They kept arguing while the man finished pulling the saddle and the diaper bag out of the water. The mare and the other horse were near the bank cropping tufts of grass. Galeno waded slowly out of the river, almost fainting. The woman had unwrapped the baby's blanket, and she and the man made sure he was really all right. Then they looked at Galeno and spoke to him. They were on their way home from a party, and it had been three years since they had come over that road. They remembered that before, the river could be forded at this spot, and there wasn't so much underbrush or clay. The woman came up to Galeno, examined the wound in his shoulder, and saw the maggots in it.

"What happened to you?" she asked.

He didn't have the strength to lie, and he explained how he came to be in such a state.

"Maggots eating your flesh and you don't do anything because you're scared to get help?"

They took care of him. Rinaldo fixed up the girth strap and helped Galeno onto the horse. They took him to their small farm, the man on foot and Galeno riding. Galeno tried to thank them, to explain that trouble might come up for anyone who helped him.

"You save our son's life and you think we're going to leave you out in the woods, as bad off as you are?" the woman asked. She answered her own question: "Absolutely not."

Rinaldo told Galeno that he could rest easy at their place. Neither the police nor anyone else ever showed up unexpectedly. So Galeno stayed on the farm until his wounds healed and he felt strong again. Then he said goodbye to the couple, took the road to the river, and followed it. But he didn't go back to where his father lived. He was afraid that the police could appear anytime and arrest him. He worked along the river, helping load and unload boats. After a time he became a boatman himself and ferried people and animals back and forth across the river. He had a helper, a boy called Flavio, who rode in the prow and watched for things the boat should avoid, like stumps in the water or dead animals. When he saw something dangerous, he rang a warning bell. He pulled a string hooked up to the bell and Galeno, guiding the rudder, turned the boat right or left. Galeno lived this kind of life until his father sent a person summoning him. The father was sick and wanted to divide up the inheritance so that there wouldn't be squabbling among the children after his death.

"If you got yourself into so much trouble that you can't live here without fear of the police, then you keep the animals we raised, sell them, and stay hidden," he told Galeno.

But if Galeno thought he could live with the consequences of the wrong things he had done, he should come back, and in that case he would receive part of his father's land. Galeno came back, received the land situated beside Indian Hollow, married Betina, and had nine children. They left there only when the waters of the dam rose to cover the ranches, the roads, the trees. The waters covered the isolated country houses and the houses of the town, which were clustered together. Like the one that had remained closed ever since a tragedy occurred under its roof, a tragedy involving a man called Alceu and his wife, Mirtes. She had married another man when she was very young and had a daughter, Milena. Then she separated from her first husband and married Alceu. He was serious and introspective; Mirtes was outgoing and cheery, friendly with everyone. He worked in the bank and she took care of the house and the little girls: Milena, from her first marriage, and Mirna, the daughter she had with Alceu.

"She could read Alceu's thoughts," her mother said later. When Mirna was four years old, Mirtes wanted to get a job, and Alceu helped her to find one at the bank where he worked. She soon proved herself an excellent public-relations woman and made friends with everyone. Their financial situation improved; they bought things, started to go to dinners and birthday parties, and she was always the liveliest, most interesting woman there. She continued to do whatever Alceu wanted, but he thought that when they made love, she sometimes seemed distracted. He began to feel insecure. He couldn't imagine another woman as beautiful, as attractive or companionable as Mirtes, and he thought that other men wanted her as much as he did. The parties and dinners soon ceased to be fun and started to annoy him. He stopped going to them, but he didn't see why he should impose limitations on his wife. He would tell her to go and make an excuse for his absence. At times she was reluctant.

"It's disagreeable. I'm your wife but I always go alone," she said. "I don't feel right."

"Go on," he would tell her. "You enjoy parties and you should."

Her way of dressing, which was informal and in good taste, began to bother him, too. He would control himself, but when he was alone, he would mutter, "She wants to show herself off to someone. She wants to look even prettier."

The two of them would talk at night in their bedroom, and when they did, he would understand how groundless his annoyance and suspicion were. But it hurt him to see the differences between them.

"I'm limiting you, both in your relationships with other people and in your work," he started to say.

She told him that he was wrong, he wasn't limiting her.

"I just need to adapt myself to your habits."

But one night she didn't reassure him as usual, but kept

quiet, which left Alceu hurt and bitter. Another time, in their room, when he repeated that he was limiting her, Mirtes agreed.

"Yes, actually, in a way I do feel limited."

Then she fell silent and Alceu realized that her love for him had cooled. It was as if a dagger had stabbed deep into his chest, because he couldn't accept the idea of not being the most important thing in Mirtes's life. He thought about their conversation for several days, decided he was losing her, and concluded that the best thing would be for them to separate. He proposed the separation to her and they discussed the subject without argument, without anger, both agreeing, in the end, that this was the best solution. The two of them were lying down, and he felt an immense emptiness inside himself because Mirtes hadn't disagreed with his reasoning. She had accepted his proposal instead. They planned everything together: how the girls should be told, when he would leave the house, how they would divide up their property. Then he went to look in a dresser drawer for some business papers. Mirtes lay back against the pillows and from time to time he looked in her direction and saw her, pensive and a little sad, wearing only a bra and panties, as he liked her to do when they were alone in the bedroom. He thought how beautiful she was and suddenly realized that it would be impossible for him to live without her. The idea of losing her was insupportable. In the drawer he was pawing through was a revolver. He removed it from its cover, turned toward Mirtes, and shot in the direction of her face. He shot once, twice, three times. She was thrown back against the headboard by the impact of the bullets. A great tenderness invaded him for the woman whose lifeblood was draining out of her. He looked into her sightless eyes, lay down across her still-warm legs, placed the barrel of the revolver in his ear, and killed himself.

The girls and the maid were asleep and didn't hear the shots. The next morning when neither Mirtes nor Alceu showed up at work, a colleague went to their house and learned that they were locked inside the bedroom. He knocked a few times at the door, got no answer, and decided to call Mirtes's parents. When they arrived, Milena, the eleven-year-old, was trying to get the key out of the lock on the other side, using a bobby pin. They sent the child away, broke down the door, and found the two in the position in which they had died. Mirtes's father took the girls to live with him and didn't want to rent or sell the house. It was closed up. When the waters covered the city, he and his wife were still trying to understand what had happened between their daughter and son-in-law inside that room.

And the waters also covered the ranch of a man called Dalton, but known as Sharpshooter because his left eyelid drooped, covering half his eye. One day when he was a boy, he wanted to shoot a cat and made himself a pistol that exploded the first time he fired it. He made the barrel from the handle of an old umbrella, taking care to do everything just right. The breech, hammer, and sights were tied tightly onto the barrel. He put in plenty of gunpowder, followed by the wadding, which he tamped down hard. Then came the birdshot and the blasting caps. When he tested the gun by shooting at a board, the barrel exploded and the hammer came loose, hitting him above one eye.

After that the lid drooped as if his eye were half-closed, so people always called him Sharpshooter. Adjacent to his ranch were the lands belonging to Sr. Cicero, who was married to Rosália. She was a woman of strong temperament, always attentive to things, complaining about what was wrong, correcting other people's defects. She was irascible and swore a lot but Cicero couldn't get along without her help. He liked everything neat and tidy, but he was the first to mess up whatever was near him. He would come in the living room with manure and mud on his feet, throw his hat on the bed, forget to close the screen door after him.

"Cicero," she would say, "come back and clean those feet."

"Cicero, don't throw your sweaty hat on top of the bed."

"Close the door, look at the mosquitoes!"

And he would take his hat off the bed. Muttering, he would go back to clean off his feet and close the screen door so the mosquitoes wouldn't take over the house. He liked corn pudding, chicken cooked in blood-and-vinegar sauce, meat with zucchini. These things only came out right when Rosália supervised their preparation. He tried to be friendly with others, but didn't know how to relate to people very well, not even his own relatives. One of his brothers would come to visit occasionally and he wouldn't know how to act. He would wake early and, instead of going out to take care of the ranch, stay home so as not to leave the brother alone. The brother got up late, took a nap after lunch, and spent most of his time with his nose in a book. Cicero felt it would be rude to leave the house, and the brother in turn felt ill at ease. Cicero would wake him up, interrupt his reading to talk of the crops, the cows, the workers.

Then Rosália would resolve the problem, saying, "Go on out and take care of your work, I'll keep him company."

It was Rosália who showed him how to talk with an employee, how to get around any misunderstanding caused by his clumsy manner of dealing with people. She pointed out the people he could trust.

"It's better to ask Dona Florinda to deliver that message." Or: "Send Sidney to make the payment."

Every night a rosary was prayed, and it was then that Rosália gathered her information. Surrounded by her maids, she would wait for the moments between prayers and then ask about the work being done on the ranch, give orders, advise. Natércia, the housemaid, would unbraid her hair, brush it out, and braid it up again, whispering into her ear everything that was happening. Rosália would correct errors, demand that orders be carried out, control people. But they all went to her when they needed help.

Cicero would say, "She's got her finger in every pie."

Sometimes he would call to a worker and she would announce, "He's in the corral," or "He's taking serum out to the pigpen."

If he complained that a worker was slow she would say, "It's not his fault. He hurt his knee on the gate and can't walk any faster."

"Nadile is crying because her husband got drunk last night and they had a fight."

Among the women who worked in the house, only Zeli, Natércia's daughter, could wash and starch the shirts and linens to suit Rosália. The mother and daughter lived there on the ranch and Zeli, besides washing and ironing, made brown-sugar candy and cooked very well. But she was approaching thirty and hadn't married yet. On the ranch there was a cowhand named Orestes, very thin, ugly, and timid with girls.

Cicero, who always praised his work, remarked one day, "Orestes is going to quit."

"I know," Rosália answered.

Cicero asked her if she could figure out some way of keeping him on the ranch.

"If he wants to leave, it's better to let him go."

"But he's the best help I have. I can't get along without him," said Cicero.

A few days later he asked her to go with him to the edge of the ranch where he had ordered a bridge built. Rosália didn't like to ride through the pastures, but Cicero insisted so much that she couldn't ignore him.

"I need your opinion," he argued.

The two mounted their horses, but before they could get halfway there they met Virgilino, a worker who told them, "Damsel fell into the quicksand."

The cow had broken through the fence around the slough, fallen in, and gotten stuck.

"Orestes sent me to get another lasso," Virgilino explained.

Cicero and Rosália rode to the slough. When they got there, Damsel had sunk in halfway up her legs. She grunted, making an effort to get out, but couldn't budge an inch.

When she saw them, she began to toss her head, and Cicero commented, "It's going to be hard to get her out."

"How did she get so far into the middle?" Rosália wanted to know.

"She must have been frightened by something," he answered.

Orestes was a little way off, sitting on the ground, his horse grazing near a thicket. He signaled for them not to come any closer, got up, and walked over, explaining that Damsel was very agitated and it wasn't good for anyone to get near her. She would just struggle harder and waste more strength. He showed them the place in the fence where she had broken through and said that he would try to pull her out of the quicksand from the other side with the help of two lassos.

"She's sunk too far in to turn around and go back," he explained.

Cicero and Orestes talked some more, and Rosália rode her horse into the shade of a tree and watched the cow. She had the impression that little by little, each time Damsel shook her head, she sank deeper. When Virgilino came back with the rope, Orestes took his own lasso, plus the second one, and went into the fenced-off area. Cicero and Virgilino went around to the other side.

"You stay here," Cicero said to Rosália. "Damsel will come out of there mighty angry, ready to horn somebody."

Rosália dismounted and watched from the shady spot under the tree. The cow tossed her horns when she saw Orestes approaching, but couldn't move anything besides her head and neck. He lassoed her horns and threw the end of the rope to Virgilino, who tied it to his saddle. Then Virgilino spurred his horse to keep the rope taut, not letting Damsel turn her head and gouge Orestes, who jumped on her back and tied the other rope around her belly. To do this, he had to get into the quicksand up to his shoulders, leaving only his face above the surface.

"Quiet, hold still!" he told the animal.

Then he threw the end of the second rope to Cicero, who also tied it to his saddle horn. The two horses started to strain, pulling the cow.

"Come on, Damsel! Let's go!" Orestes yelled.

But she didn't move. Orestes grabbed her tail and bent it upward, shouting, "Get going, Damsel! Come on!"

Because of the pain, she tried to fight back and managed to advance a little, just over one handspan. They kept on that way, hauling on the two ropes, Orestes yelling and twisting the cow's tail. She felt pain, struggled and advanced a few inches at a time. Finally her hooves touched hard bottom and she could support her own weight. She burst out of the quicksand with horns lowered, ready to attack anything that moved. Cicero and Virgilino kept the horses away, tightening their ropes so she couldn't get near either one of them. Orestes, out of the mud now, called to her, calming her down. Outside the fence they let her go, and the three men went over to where Rosália was. Orestes was cleaning the mud off his shirt, arms, and trousers.

Rosália said to him, "Give those clothes to Zeli, Natércia's daughter. She'll wash and mend them for you."

When she got home, she summoned Zeli and the two had a talk.

"Those clothes have to be very well washed, mended, and ironed," she explained. And Zeli wasn't to send them when they were ready, just to let Orestes know he should come and get them.

Zeli listened carefully and Rosália rehearsed her on what to say to Orestes, how to praise his efforts and hard work. "And tell him that from now on you'll take care of washing his clothes."

Zeli was also to let him know she was happy about this. Rosália told her at what point she should invite him in, insist he have a seat in the living room, when to offer him coffee and cake.

Zeli listened carefully and answered, "Yes, ma'am."

She listened and followed Rosália's instructions to the letter. Before long she and Orestes were sweethearts. By the time they had the wedding date set, he had already been told many times (and was in complete agreement) that he couldn't quit his job because Natércia wouldn't hear of leaving the ranch herself, nor of her daughter's moving far away.

Bordering Cicero and Rosália's land lived Lídio Alves. A strange thing occurred in his house one day. His wife was called Elida Alves, and they had one girl and three boys. The oldest child died when he was seven years old. He felt a strong pain in his stomach, cried out, clutched his belly, and died. They prepared a coffin, put it in the living room, and when it was almost time for the funeral, the boy sat up. Seeing people crying all around him, he started to cry, too. The people were frightened and some of them ran away. But Elida and Lídio Alves hugged their son and took him to his bedroom. He said he was nauseated with the smell of the flowers and felt hungry. They took the flowers out of the house and Dona Elida went to the kitchen and made some cornmeal mush. The boy ate it and got well.

Nearby was another ranch called White Water, which was the property of Sr. Petersen, a man who had come from the south with his wife, Idalecia, and their two children. Rainer, the son, was the younger. The daughter was named Valdeneide and was thin and nervous. Sr. Petersen came from the south, bought White Water and another ranch in the valley called Crying Boy. He set up a beef-salting operation on White Water and used both ranches to breed cattle and fatten them. A crystal mine was discovered on Crying Boy but he paid no attention to it; he was only interested in the cows and the salt beef. He milked the cows and fattened the steers for slaughter, cut the slabs of meat, salted it, and made jerky. Rainer grew up learning his father's work. When he was sixteen or eighteen, Sr. Petersen took an interest in the crystal mine. He began to abandon the cows and the beef salting and spent more time on Crying Boy. With his absence, things began to go wrong at White Water, but he didn't care, he hardly noticed them. He was only interested in extracting crystal and playing around with the women he always found in those parts.

Rainer discovered the wrongdoings and said, "Father, they're stealing from us."

But he didn't care. All he wanted was to putter around at the crystal mine, roast goats, drink, and chase women. So Rainer began to assume responsibility for White Water. He cracked down on the workers and put the beef-salting operation in order, firing an employee here, another there. When his mother needed something, she asked him. His father would go off for weeks on end, only sending word when he needed money or supplies. Some of the workers who had gotten used to taking all the milk they wanted or going into the slaughterhouse and helping themselves to meat, blood, and bones to sell weren't very happy. Rainer began to hear that so-and-so wanted to kill him, that somebody else had sworn to see him dead, that they were going to set an ambush and attack him. He paid no attention to the threats, but he heard so many angry rumors that one day he called a meeting in the workers' barracks. When everyone who worked on the ranch was assembled and waiting, he came in wearing a cape that covered him from his shoulders to the floor. Under it he carried a carbine next to his body. He walked back and forth saying that he had heard many of them were unhappy, that certain people even wanted to kill him. So he intended to make one thing clear: he was the boss here, their chief. He was in charge, and things had to be done as he ordered. Whoever didn't like it, whoever didn't agree with his rules, could ask for their wages and leave at once.

"But if you stay, you have to do your work right."

Moreover, he didn't want to hear any more of this nonsense about people wanting to kill him, shoot him dead.

"If anyone has anything against me, let's settle it right now."

He said that, and nobody answered. And the uncooperativeness stopped, the threats and the rumors of ambush. Things began to run smoothly and his profits grew. He lived at White Water with his mother and sister, but his father stayed on at the crystal mine, drinking and sending for money and supplies every so often. Rainer's mother took care of the house and Valdeneide stayed inside her room, always nervous and at times prophesying things that were going to happen in the future. Rainer didn't believe in her predictions, but lots of people did. One day she said that a certain pasture would catch fire, and a week hadn't gone by before it did. She would say that a person was going to get sick because she had dreamed about that person suffering a great deal, and the person ended up getting sick. She would look at the belly of a pregnant woman, and if she said the unborn child was a boy, you could be certain it would be. She lived quietly inside her room, which was extremely clean. If she found the slightest speck of dirt, she would have an attack of nerves and a maid would have to be called to clean whatever she said was dirty.

Whenever Sr. Petersen showed up at White Water, he arrived in a noisy manner, talking loud, always bringing several of his workers from the mine and wanting nothing to do with cows, steers, or beef jerky. He always wanted to have a barbecue and get drunk. One afternoon he sent a message saying that he would be there the next day with an accordion player, a guitar player, and fifteen more men, and Rainer should prepare a party. When he got there with the men, the accordion player and guitar player, he found everything prepared. The patio was clean, the drinks and glasses laid out, and cuts of meat for barbecuing lay on the table, seasoned and ready.

"All set," Rainer told him.

Sr. Petersen looked around and asked, "Didn't I say it was to be a party?"

"But I prepared everything," Rainer answered. "What's missing?"

"The girls!"

"What girls?"

"To dance, silly, whoever saw a party without girls?"

Sr. Petersen thought awhile and then summoned the women who worked in the house. Rainer warned the married ones to stay hidden and only the single ones came, of which there were three. His father looked at the three and said, "Call Valdeneide, too."

She was nervous and never left her room but she was afraid of her father, who paid no attention to her affectations, so she obeyed him at once.

"You're going to dance," he ordered.

Silent, clumsy, and skinny, she stayed there, dancing with the men from the mine, along with the three other girls. At times, during the intervals when the music stopped, she would come up to her father and ask, "May I go back to my room now?"

"It's still early," he would answer, and order the musicians to start up the music again. The four girls danced as long as the party lasted. They danced with one of the men, taking turns, as long as Sr. Petersen thought the party should continue.

Rainer took care of the cows and the beef salting and kept his eye on a girl called Nancy, who lived nearby. She was the daughter of Oldeivo, a strait laced Protestant who was extremely strict with Nancy and her two sisters. He went out at night to prayer meetings and would not allow his daughters to have boyfriends. He locked them in the house, always saying it was too early for them to be thinking of such things. Rainer went to speak with him, told him his intentions, and asked his permission to court Nancy. Oldeivo found this a great offense and kept an even tighter rein on his daughter. He even forbade her to come to the door of the house. He knew all about Sr. Petersen and supposed that Rainer must be like his father. So Rainer eloped with the girl. It was on a dark night. He drove his pickup truck to a point near the house, got out, and went to meet Nancy. She climbed out the window, he wrapped her in his long cape, and the two walked in the direction of the pickup. They had already planned everything with the help of some other people. But when they were leaving the house, Oldeivo appeared on his way home from prayer meeting. They passed him, and taking advantage of the dark, Rainer silently raised his hand and tipped his hat in greeting. From his horse, Oldeivo nodded back from his horse, not knowing who was greeting him nor noticing that there were four feet sticking out below the cape. The two went on to the truck, drove to White Water, where Dona Idalecia, Valdeneide, and one of Oldeivo's sisters were waiting. They prepared Nancy, and when the sun rose, they all went to town and the marriage was performed. Everything had been taken care of and the priest performed the ceremony without knowing that the girl had run away from her father.

Only that morning did Oldeivo discover Nancy's absence. He tried to make the other girls tell him where she had gone, but they only answered, "We don't know, Father. We didn't see anything."

They kept denying all knowledge until the time when the marriage was over. Then they decided to tell him, for Nancy and Rainer would already be married and on their way back to White Water, where they set up house. Oldeivo was very angry and said he was going to teach Rainer a lesson. Other people reasoned with him, insisting that he shouldn't cause trouble. Still, he resolved to disown his daughter, saying, "Now I have only two daughters. Nancy has ceased to exist for me."

Going from these lands in the direction of the river, one passed close by a hill called São Vicente where many people lived, among them Marcos, Ivo Márcio, and Venâncio. At the top of the hill were a cross and a chapel, and on the fifteenth of August the Feast of Our Lady was commemorated there. Every year, well before August began, the host of the festival went out with his family to visit the neighbors and ask for their contributions. On the day of Our Lady, very early, lots of people would climb up the hill and set off firecrackers. A priest would come out from town to celebrate Mass. After that everyone would come down the hill to the home of whoever was host. There was always a huge barbecue with corn pudding and rum to drink, and people danced until morning.

The year that Ivo Márcio's name was drawn as host of the feast, he complained about the contributions, saying that they weren't enough to cover the expenses.

He calculated the quantity of meat he had received and concluded, "That won't be enough for everyone."

So he bought two young, lean steers from Venâncio. They haggled over the price a long while, Ivo Márcio saying it was too high and Venâncio saying it was too low: "I'm only charging you this because it's for the Feast of Our Lady."

They couldn't agree on the weight of the steers, either. Venâncio judged that together they weighed eight hundred and eighty pounds, but Ivo Márcio calculated seven hundred and fifty pounds. "At most," he affirmed.

They finally agreed on four hundred and ten pounds per steer and closed the deal. But on the day of the feast, Ivo Márcio called Venâncio over to the shed where the women were preparing the skewers of meat and said, "Look at that. Tell me if there's enough meat there for two steers weighing four hundred and ten pounds each."

He pointed out the huge clay dishes with the cuts of meat ready to be barbecued. They went back to arguing over the weight and price, while the women kept on preparing the skewers, the *farofa* of manioc flour and scrambled eggs, the cans of juice. Ivo Márcio was nervous because it was still very early, but people were already arriving, coming into the yard. He looked at the big crowd gathering and feared there would never be enough food and drink, because some of the men were already demanding rum and the women and children wanted fruit juice.

He interrupted his discussion and complained, "How can you be wanting to drink already? The Mass hasn't even been said yet!"

He said that the people shouldn't be there, they had to wait up on top of the hill, near the cross.

"The party's afterward," he repeated.

One of his sons came up and told him that the other son, the youngest, had filled the barbecue pit up with water.

"They told him to dampen the charcoal before lighting it, and he got the hose and soaked it all down."

Someone else came to advise him that the pickup with the barrels of beer had broken an axle coming over a culvert and they needed another car to go and get the barrels. His daughter came to say that his wife was asking if they should put people in charge of serving the food, or if everyone was to serve himself mayonnaise salad and *farofa*. Also, she had no idea where the crates with the cutlery and plates had gotten to. In the yard, young men and girls were dancing to loud music from a car radio.

"The Mass hasn't been said yet, folks," Ivo Márcio repeated, nervous.

Soon the priest came and sought out Ivo Márcio. He turned his back on all these things, got into the car with his wife, Moema, his daughter, and the priest, and they headed for the chapel. When they got to the top of the hill, everything was decorated. Ivo Nárcio was happy with the work that Moema, his daughter, and some neighbor ladies had done during the night, arranging paper flowers and hanging streamers of paper flags. They had worked until very late cutting out colored tissue-paper triangles and gluing them to the string to make the streamers. Before sunup they climbed the hill to tie the streamers up on bamboo rods stuck into the ground and glue the paper flowers to the arms of the cross. They came back complaining that their hands were freezing, but the job had to be done early in the morning so that the mists and humidity of the night wouldn't unglue everything. And there was also the problem of the ladder that was too short to reach the place where the paper flowers were supposed to go. So they had to get somebody's truck, take it up close to the tall cross, and put the ladder on top of the truck bed. But in spite of all this, when Ivo Márcio got to the top of the hill and saw the colored streamers, the happy crowd surrounding the chapel, and the altar raised at the foot of the cross, he thought everything looked beautiful and well prepared. They had put an altar near the cross because all those people would never fit inside the chapel.

During the Mass, the priest gave a long sermon about Our Lady and told the history of the little church, remembering other festivals. From time to time he stopped to call people closer to the altar. He said a lot of things that Ivo Márcio didn't think were the slightest bit necessary.

"Come closer, up here by me," the priest said. "Don't be afraid, I'm not a wolf, I'm the pastor of the sheep."

"Can't he see that the sun is too hot for all this talk?" Ivo Márcio commented under his breath to Moema.

After the sermon came to the end and the priest finished the Mass, people started leaving. They spread out, going down the hill toward Ivo Márcio's house. Some were on foot, others had cars. The priest, surrounded by a group of the faithful, talked calmly as he took off his vestments and white tunic, put away the chalice and the spatula in a bag. Slowly, still surrounded by his flock, he walked to Ivo Márcio's car. They went down the hill, passing cars and pickup trucks stuck in holes or with tires punctured by sharp sticks. Ivo Márcio knew the roads well and had no difficulty getting back. When they arrived, the priest continued to talk as if everyone inside the car had the whole day to hear his stories. Ivo Márcio called Nívio, his brother, set him down beside the priest to hear the stories, and went to see about the party. He spent the day attending to people and resolving problems. He judged it would be best to give out the food and drink little by little, but it proved a struggle.

Lines were formed and many people complained and swore.

"What a miserable party!" they said.

At nightfall Ivo Márcio changed his mind. "Serve until everything's gone," he ordered. "Maybe when there's nothing left, these people will clear out of here."

But the crowd didn't diminish. Every time he thought it would, he looked at the road leading to the ranch and saw more headlights on the road, coming toward them. Much later, it grew cold and people gathered wood, made bonfires in the front and back of the house, and danced around them. At one point someone came to tell Ivo Márcio that the meat was gone and he remembered two cans of pork that his neighbor, Luis Fernando, had sent that afternoon. His brother had put them away. He went to look for Nívio and found him in the kitchen beside the stove, taking an ear of corn from the embers. He had a fork in one hand, poking the coals, and his other hand was grabbing the legs of Dona Maria Augusta, the wife of Valdomiro, who owned the Blue Rock Ranch. She was perfectly quiet, with Nívio's hand on her leg, waiting for the ear of corn. Ivo Márcio called his brother and told him to take the cans of pork out to the barbecue pit. The drinks were gone but every minute someone would produce a bottle of rum which was immediately passed from mouth to mouth. A neighbor called José Guilherme, who had sent three sacks of potatoes and all the eggs for the *farofa* and mayonnaise salad, sent word that he was going home because he wasn't feeling well. He had a toothache that had flared up all of a sudden, and he said good night together with his wife and two daughters. Ivo Márcio saw that he was quite sick and told his brother to take him home.

"You can use my car," he said to Nívio. And he told José Guilherme, "You can come get yours tomorrow when you feel better."

José Guilherme tried to say that it wasn't necessary, but his wife broke in, "No, it's better if Nívio takes us."

Ivo Márcio accompanied them to the car, they got in, and Nívio drove off with them. Going back up the steps, he passed Dona Maria Augusta, who was coming down them. She smiled as if he hadn't seen anything unusual in the kitchen. He turned and took a furtive look at her legs. Pretty legs, well made, legs he had always admired but never imagined trying to touch.

And that damn Nívio runs the stoplight, he thought to himself.

It was late, but the party was still going strong. Even after the pork was gone, and the corn pudding, *farofa*, and mayonnaise salad, people continued dancing around the bonfires. Long after midnight, Ivo Márcio called Moema and his daughter in and they closed the doors of their bedrooms. Ivo Márcio left his sons and two employees with the guests and went to sleep. He didn't see his brother until the next day at lunchtime, when Nívio was getting back.

Nívio told him, "José Guilherme's dead."

Ivo Márcio was greatly shocked.

"Dead! But how?"

Nívio explained that they hadn't gone back to José Guilherme's ranch. "We went directly to the city." José Guilherme couldn't even talk, he was in so much pain.

"We went to get a doctor."

In the hospital the doctor who examined him said at once that it was his heart.

"Was it his tooth or his heart?" asked Ivo Márcio.

"His tooth," answered Nívio. "He only felt pain in his tooth, but the problem was with his heart."

Nívio said that right there in the hospital José Guilherme grew worse and died. He had spent the rest of the night and part of the morning helping to contact the relatives and friends.

"When I left, the hospital was full of people crying."

They were in the hall, in the waiting room, all saying that they couldn't believe what had happened. An uncle of José Guilherme's, an old man almost eighty, sat down on the steps and said that life wasn't worth a damn. That a person could work and work, and from one minute to the next just die without warning.

"He was shouting that José Guilherme had worked his whole life without stopping, and now this had happened. He died for no reason at all," Nívio related.

But the waters came and covered up the chapel, the cross, and all the houses. Not only those near São Vicente Hill, but all the houses on all the ranches, the houses in the villages and the city. Like the one belonging to Sr. Venilton, who was a tax collector and had once been hopeful that his wife, Adelaine, would be named director of the state-supported school. He wrote to the congressman Goytá Resendo, whom he had met during his campaign, and after some time the congressman sent him a telegram saying that the following Sunday he would be on board the *President Wenceslau*, the riverboat that passed through the city every two weeks. The boat would be in port from eleven to two o'clock; the congressman suggested that they have lunch together. Venilton told Adelaine to prepare the best lunch she possibly could, for at least ten people, because, as he said, congressmen never traveled alone. Adelaine sent for two cooks and one confectioner, all reliable, and they decided what would be served, and on the day the congressman was supposed to come, they prepared a variety of dishes and innumerable desserts, all of the best quality, beautifully served up and garnished. Promptly that morning Venilton went to wait for the arrival of the *President Wenceslau*. He saw the boat appear way up at the curve of the river, waited for it to dock, and watched the passengers come down, but he didn't see the congressman. Then he went on board and asked the captain, who didn't know Goytá Resendo. Venilton described him as being tall and thin, with a mustache.

"The only tall thin man is a dentist," said the captain. "But he doesn't wear a mustache."

He consulted the list of passengers who were on board and confirmed, "He's not on the list."

Then he enumerated the people who had just gotten off: six men, two women, and the dentist who was called Casimiro Abelha, accompanied by his wife, five small children, and a maid.

"It's that fellow there with the family," said the captain, referring to a man who below, on the dockside, was carrying suitcases to a rental car.

The captain commented, "He's moving here to live."

Venilton mentioned the congressman's telegram.

"Something else must have come up so he couldn't make it."

"Yes, that must be it," agreed Venilton.

As he was leaving he passed by the dentist, who was arranging for an extra rental car. The man, one of his daughters, and the driver were loading the car with luggage. The first car had already gone on with his wife, the maid, and the rest of the children. The little girl lost her balance as she lugged a large bag and Venilton took it from her hands and brought it to the trunk of the car.

"Oh, thank you so much," said the dentist.

He introduced himself, saying his name and profession and explaining that he was arriving with his family to take up residence in the city. He and his wife had been there a month ago and acquired a very comfortable house, which would do perfectly as a residence. He planned to transform the two front bedrooms into his consulting office.

"It's on Padre Paradise Street, number thirty," he added.

Venilton said that it was a pleasure to meet him and said good-bye rather absently. He went to the office of a fellow party member to see if there was any news of the congressman. The person couldn't tell him anything and asked why Venilton wanted to know.

Venilton told him about Goytá Resendo's telegram, adding, "But he didn't come in on the *President Wenceslau*."

"Something must have come up, some last-minute conflict."

"Yes, it must be," Venilton agreed.

Then he went to advise his wife that there wouldn't be any lunch. As he crossed Padre Paradise Street, two streets before his own, he saw the dentist's house. The man was carrying suitcases from the porch to the living room, the windows were open, and you could see the children trotting back and forth inside.

When Adelaine learned that Goytá Resendo hadn't arrived, she said, "But didn't he tell us he was coming today?"

"Yes, but he's not here," answered Venilton.

"But what will we do with all this food?"

"Why, eat it, and what's left over we'll send to somebody else."

Adelaine lamented the trouble they had gone to and, looking at the table set for ten people, told the maid to start putting away the plates and silverware.

"Wait a minute," interrupted Venilton. And he told her about the dentist. Then he sent his fourteen-year-old daughter over to Padre Paradise Street with a message for Dr. Casimiro Abelha. She was to say they were inviting him and his family to lunch. They knew what a hard job moving was, and the difficulties of getting settled in a new place, and they were inviting them to eat.

"Say that your mother and I insist that they all come to our house. Dr. Abelha, his wife, the children, and their maid."

The daughter was to apologize for Venilton's not going personally to get them, but he was helping with the lunch. He warned his daughter, "Wait and come back with them."

The dentist and his wife were very formal and well mannered. They were surprised at such a delicious and varied meal and didn't know how to thank their new friends. From then on they visited Venilton and Adelaine several times a year and at Christmas always stopped by to pay their respects. And Casimiro Abelha said they should bring their children to his office. But Venilton didn't like Adelaine to take them because Casimiro never charged.

"How can I charge?" he asked. "It would be an affront." In his conversations with other people he never lost an opportunity to remark, "When I came to this town, Venilton and Adelaine gave me a prince's welcome."

Next door to his house lived a woman named Cynthia, who was sixty-six years old. Her husband, Luciano, had worked at many things, and left a small bus company when he died. The company owned two buses that ran between the city and two smaller towns. Cynthia continued to manage the company in spite of her children's insistence that she give it up. Every day she worked as a conductress, traveling back and forth. The two lines connected the city to the villages of Gavião and Eugenho da Lima. The buses left in the morning, each one for one of the towns, and came back in the afternoon. The line to Gavião got back at 3:00 P.M. and the one from Eugenho da Lima at six. Every morning Cynthia would choose one of the buses, get in, and make the trip both ways, charging the passengers. It was hard to balance herself inside the bus, and when there were no seats left due to the number of passengers that boarded along the route, she rode standing up, bumping against the backs of the seats. Lots of people got on and off along the route to go shorter distances, and she had to pay attention so that they didn't get off without paying. Her children kept insisting that she give up these trips, or at least let the conductors do the work. But she said that it was the only way of controlling the bus lines. Traveling and charging, without anybody being sure which bus she would choose to take, she could control things better. Like how many people took the bus, the proper observance of the timetable, the treatment the drivers gave the passengers.

"Nobody steals from me, I keep an eye on everything," she would say.

The roads were not paved, and during the rainy season the trips usually took much longer. If it got dark, she had to be very careful not to mix up the bills. Even so, she didn't stop riding the buses and acting as conductress. The passengers carried everything under the sun. There was a fixed price per piece of luggage, whether it was a chicken, a roll of wire, a bundle of firewood, or a basketful of groceries. When the packages weren't stashed securely in place, they would roll through the aisle and Cynthia had to duck behind a seat or find a way to fold her legs up so she wouldn't be hit. Once a roll of barbed wire came loose as they were going up a hill and a man caught it to keep her from getting hurt. He cut his fingers and ripped his shirt sleeve. Then he demanded that the owner of the barbed wire pay for his shirt. They came to the point of pulling out knives to settle their differences, and she had to beg them for the love of God not to fight. Another time it was a bundle of wood that got loose near the seats and scratched the boots of one of the passengers. He screamed that the boots were brand new and he wanted the owner of the firewood to pay for a new pair. They argued, too, and got off the bus punching each other. Cynthia ordered the baggage to be put into the racks, but at times they would get too full, and you couldn't leave the people on the roads with the things they were carrying. Her children, when they found out about the fights, or when the rains covered the roads with mud, would once more insist that she give up the work, but Cynthia wouldn't hear of it. She had always been a strong-willed woman.

"Your father called me stubborn," she commented.

She and Luciano had had two children who gave her a lot of trouble coming into the world. Both times she thought she couldn't stand feeling so nauseated. From the beginning of each pregnancy to the end she felt sick.

"You two were alike in only one way," she liked to say.

Aside from that they had never been alike at all. Luciano never got involved with them, and she had to take care of all their needs. The older, Paulo Henrique, was as methodical as clockwork from the start. He would nurse exactly every three hours and later, when he was older, he continued to get hungry at the same intervals. Even at night he would say he was hungry, and he was a very sturdy boy. With Jonathan, the second, she tried everything to get him on a schedule, but it was no use. He never had regular habits, and it was a waste of time to force him to eat, because he just threw everything up again. He would only eat when he decided to. Paulo Henrique loved bananas baked in milk and any kind of soup, but Jonathan couldn't stand either soup or bananas. Jonathan would spend hours puttering about alone. Sometimes she would go looking for him because she hadn't seen him anywhere for hours and would find him very quiet, entertaining himself with some game. She tried to make her children more similar, but her efforts brought so few results that in the end she gave up. She imagined that they were difficult to change because they had been born boys. Luciano once got himself a dog that had the habit of going off and spending ten or fifteen days away. Then it would come back and calmly install itself again in the corner of the kitchen. At lunchtime and dinnertime it would go over to the door and wait to be served its food. The dog wasn't fond of children, and in exchange Cynthia wasn't very friendly with the dog. Even so, when it arrived thin and unkempt from its periods of absence, she would worry. She couldn't understand why, having a corner with food and water, the dog would go away for so long.

Luciano would say, "He's out womanizing."

"Why can't he womanize and come back every day?"

"He has his reasons," Luciano answered, finding it all very natural.

Luciano was gratified with the presence of the dog but never even stroked it or took any trouble to keep it from disappearing. When Luciano first brought it home, Cynthia liked to feed it, but when the dog bit her fingers as it reached quickly for a piece of meat, she began to be afraid of the animal. She was revolted by that gaping mouth advancing and snapping up the food she offered.

"He has unpredictable reactions," she said. "Some of his owner's habits must have rubbed off on him."

The dog always stayed in his corner near the stove and took no notice of her when she ordered him away from there. He only obeyed Luciano. One day when he was getting older, he went off and never came back. And Luciano, though he liked the dog's presence in the house, found it natural that he should disappear and didn't lift a finger to discover where he might be.

Cynthia had no brothers, only three sisters, and her father had died when she was still very young. Thus she grew up without knowing much about men. Her mother oriented her before she married, saying that men were very much like children.

"You have to treat your husband as if he were a little boy."

Cynthia did just that, but she soon perceived that there was a certain degree of madness in men, too. One afternoon not long after their marriage, they went to the orchard to eat mangoes. He climbed up the tree, got the best ones, and threw them down for her to catch. She sat peeling them over her outspread skirt and put them on top of a bench under the tree. When Luciano climbed down, they sat there eating the mangoes. He peeled some more for both of them with his knife, and she enjoyed being there with him. Then Luciano said he needed to go out and asked her to go back to the house.

"Let's stay here a little longer," she proposed.

Luciano said he needed to go out and take care of some business. He gave her the knife.

"You stay, then," he said.

But Cynthia wanted them both to stay. "Climb up and get me some more mangoes," she said as if she were talking to a child.

"Climb up yourself," he answered.

She grabbed him by the hand, wanting to keep him there, but he shook her loose and turned to leave.

"All right," Cynthia agreed. "But you have to carry me in your arms to the kitchen."

"I can't, I'm late as it is," Luciano told her, already a few paces off.

"If you don't carry me back, I'll never set foot inside that house again."

He didn't answer. He left and she ate a few more mangoes and decided to stay under the mango tree. Luciano came back and, not finding her, went out to the orchard.

"Are you still here?"

"I'm only going in if you carry me in."

"What nonsense!"

He turned his back, leaving her sitting on the bench. The day was waning and Cynthia didn't leave the orchard. When night came, she lay down on the bench and curled herself up, her hands and face sticky with mango juice. It grew colder, and she huddled there until the insects began to crawl over her arms and legs, and then she got up and went into the house, crying with rage.

Luciano was in the living room trying to fix an alarm clock and he asked her, "Aren't you going to fix supper?"

Cynthia didn't answer. She went into the bedroom and locked the door. Later he called her.

"What's this nonsense? Open the door."

She didn't answer, and she realized that he was forcing against the door with his shoulder but couldn't get it open. Then he called her again. She remained silent, listening to him try his strength against the door. Once again he called and she didn't answer. After a while she heard a great thudding noise: Luciano chopping through the door with an ax. Greatly alarmed, she sprang up and crouched against the wall, afraid of being hit by one of the splinters of wood that were flying about. He chopped down the door, took off his clothes, and lay down as she inched her way out of the room.

But before she could get through the door he yelled, "Come back here and lie down!"

He shouted in a way that made her go back to the bed, thinking that she had married a man subject to fits of madness. And as the years passed, her impression was confirmed. Depending on what happened to him, he really did have crazy spells. Later she saw that it wasn't just him, but all men who were subject to such fits. Like the two on the bus who wanted to kill each other with knives because of a slightly torn shirt sleeve. And the others in a fistfight because the bundle of firewood scratched the boots. To Cynthia men were beings subject to an instinct outside any rational explanation. Their impulses were not dictated by good sense.

One day Luciano sold a car. But someone came to tell him that the buyer wanted to go back on the deal.

Outraged, Luciano said between his teeth, "If he tries to back out of the deal I'll give him a bellyful of lead."

"Why, Luciano?"

It was because the man had insinuated that Luciano had put bananas in the differential of the car so that nobody could tell it was going bad. "To disguise the noise."

"Well, did you?"

He wouldn't be capable of such a thing, but she asked him nevertheless.

"Of course not, woman! Don't you know me better than that?"

"So why don't you go and talk with the man, try to clear the whole thing up?"

"Talk to that son of a bitch? A person who doesn't trust me?"

And during the next four days he went around armed with a revolver.

"If I meet him in the street and he looks at me sideways, he's going to get a bellyful of lead."

When Luciano came home in the afternoon, he would sit down in the living room, put the revolver and a box of bullets on the table, and wait for the man to appear.

"I've got ammunition enough here to finish off fifty like him," he would say without moving from his spot in front of the door.

The children were small, Jonathan only six. He came over from the corner where he was playing and asked, "Is lead soft or hard, Father?"

"It's hard, very hard," Luciano said.

And there was nothing Cynthia could do. She only prayed that no one would appear to insinuate that Luciano was dishonest. The car buyer didn't show up, and during the afternoons and evenings of those four days her husband sat there, crossing and uncrossing his legs, pulling the box of bullets closer, verifying the distance they were from his hand.

Every so often he repeated, "I've got ammunition enough to finish off fifty of his kind."

The man didn't show up, and on the fifth day Luciano got up, went out, and returned home whistling, calm.

She asked him, "Did you settle the business of the car?"

"It's settled," he answered.

"What happened?"

"It's settled," he repeated.

And he said nothing more about the matter. She could

not comprehend what good his exaggerated behavior had done. "Wasn't it just a misunderstanding?" she asked herself. "Why all the uproar?"

Cynthia became more and more convinced: "That's it. When something that's natural in him isn't satisfied, he gets unbalanced. And he can't go for long with things unbalanced inside him."

She learned to live with him when she came to accept many of his actions as attacks of madness. Even in their lovemaking she was hurt a great deal until she understood that she couldn't hope for him to change. He was the way he was. His caresses, his attentions were directed not exactly toward her, but toward the woman at his side who, due to certain attributes, aroused his interest sometimes more, sometimes less.

If I were another woman, would he say the same words? His gratification over pleasure, would it be the same? she wondered. Soon she concluded that it would be. His words, his caresses, his gratification would all be the same.

Still, when she thought, Suppose he were a different man? there came to her the certainty that she would never act in the same way simply because the person would be somebody else and thus her words and caresses would be different. The love she felt was love for a definite person. If her husband were someone else, her need to give and receive affection would develop because of that man being who he was.

"And with him it's not that way," she said to herself.

This discovery seemed to condemn her to permanent loneliness. Afterward she began to see that for men, for Luciano, it must be even lonelier. She, for better or worse, would always have the object of her love, a definite person with unique features and specific defects, while he, they, would never have anyone with whom to intermingle the self.

Perhaps that's why Mother told me to treat him like a child, she thought to herself. They always need to be cared for.

Near Cynthia lived Dr. Humberto, who regularly had serious arguments with his wife. At one time he served as a police officer. When he walked down the middle of the street, everyone cleared the way to give him a wide berth. One day he came into the police station after one of his customary fights with his wife and stumbled over the chair that his assistant was forever leaving next to the door, exactly in his path. He crashed into the chair and hurt himself so badly that he hopped around holding one knee. Then, in a gesture of nervous outrage (because this wasn't the first, second, or even third time this had happened) he pulled his pistol out of his belt and fired all its bullets into the chair, deafening the office with noise and sending everyone running to find out what had happened.

Going down the street where Cynthia and Dr. Humberto lived, you came to an alley called Leaky Pipe Alley, which ended at the foot of a small hill called Boot Hill, where Selene lived. She was the mother of Acácio, a boy of twelve who sold chickens, eggs, honey, and old roosters. The chickens, eggs, and honey went to the homes where families lived and the old roosters to a bar near the river. Acácio looked like the owner of the Triumph Bakery, Sr. Valdir, who had been interested in his mother when she came there looking for a job. As soon as he saw her he was very attracted to her and hired her to work on the earliest shift. She was to knead and prepare the bread dough for the first batch of bread. His wife, Dona Aurora, was always irritated, complaining about everything, and she had pasty white skin. Selene was olive-skinned and always spoke with people in a cheerful way. In a short time Sr. Valdir began to hug and kiss her, and they began to make love before the other employees arrived. One day she got pregnant, and since she was unmarried and people were already talking, he helped her to buy the small house on the hill and let her quit her job. Selene had other affairs with other men and two more children. Acácio, who was the oldest, quit school after third grade and was a lot of help to her. He took care of his younger brothers when she was out, raised chickens, and had six beehives that he kept about half a mile from their house, in a pasture belonging to Sr. Nilton, his mother's acquaintance.

The beehives were a lot of work. Frequently an armadillo would knock one over and attack the bees, destroying the honeycombs and eating all the honey. There were also the big tropical ants to watch out for: when they appeared, Acácio smeared the feet of the hives with hot oil and put cans or tires cut crosswise full of water around the feet so the ants couldn't climb up. Sometimes he had to move the hives to a different place. But all this effort was worthwhile, because from the end of January to the beginning of September, he gathered the honey and got many, many quarts to sell from door to door, generally to the people who were his chicken-and-egg customers. He sold the hens who weren't good layers and old roosters to Sr. Garcia, owner of a bar on the riverbank. The man was Spanish, and paid Acácio very well. His chicken pastries, which were famous in the bar, took on an even better flavor and were yet more appreciated when made with the meat of the old cocks. The beer drinkers claimed that they were the best pastries in the city. Acácio bought up old roosters from miles around. Even from ranches near the town. He could get them cheap because nobody cooked them, thinking they were too tough. So he would buy them, shove them into a sack, and sell them to the Spaniard at a handsome profit. At times Selene would look at him with pride.

"He'll be rich like his father someday," she commented.

When the waters came and covered the hill, the pasture where Acácio kept the beehives, and Sr. Garcia's bar, they also covered the house of the grain broker José Flávio, who met his wife, Laura, on one of his business trips. They arrived in the city after the honeymoon on the ship *President Epitácio Pessoa*. This boat, like the *President Wenceslau*, docked at the port every two weeks. All José Flávio's family was waiting to greet the young couple with an affectionate welcome that touched Laura's heart. The riverboat docked late in the afternoon, and when they went home, their house was all lighted up and everything was in place. Some days before, Laura had sent her trousseau and José Flávio's sisters had taken it to the house where they would live, unpacked, and made sure things were in order when they arrived. They hadn't forgotten anything: the pots and pans, the canisters with staples arranged on the shelves, the vases of flowers in the windows, the biscuits and cakes, the thermos of hot coffee with milk. After welcoming them and accompanying them to their house, the family said good night and left them to themselves. They had also found a maid for them, Tanise, who was discreet and very efficient. The couple took a long time to have children, and after Caroline was born (her delivery was difficult and painful) Laura's health became more fragile. She got sick easily and José Flávio organized his work so he would no longer need to travel. Caroline was a calm child with large eyes. Due to her mother's constant illnesses she grew accustomed to playing without making noise. One night Laura got out of bed, and only when she returned to the bedroom did José Flávio realize she had gone out.

"What happened?" he asked.

"Caroline was crying."

"Is anything wrong?"

"She had a bad dream, but she's all right now."

He went back to sleep and soon awoke to find Laura once more outside the room. He could hear Caroline crying softly, the sound muffled. Laura came in.

"Go talk to her. She had a dream about you falling off of something and she's tense, afraid you'll fall again." She repeated what the child was saying: "No, Daddy, you'll fall!"

José Flávio went to Caroline's room and lay down beside her. She continued to sob and he hugged her hard. Soon she fell asleep. He remained motionless so as not to wake her and fell asleep himself, with his daughter's little arms around his neck. They stayed that way until morning. On another occasion, one of the times when Laura was in the hospital, he took her to the office. She was three years old and as he worked she toddled about near his desk, sitting on the chairs and playing with some guavas that she had brought from home. Afterward she crawled under his desk and sat curled up in a corner. Some grain buyers came in, talked with him, went out again, and she stayed beneath the desk with her guavas, an ashtray she had gotten from the coffee table near the chairs, and a metal dish where occasionally he would put grain samples. A few days later, when he pulled the window curtains open, he discovered the ashtray and the plate holding one of the guavas, now rotten. She had left his things there when she was playing and neither he nor his secretary had noticed they were missing.

Soon after Caroline was four, Laura caught a very bad flu and also took a serious fall. Things went from bad to worse. One day she called José Flávio and asked him not to let her die without going back to her native city once more. She wanted to see the room where she had spent her childhood, to look out her old window again at the view of the river's curve. For two days in a row she begged this, and José Flávio joked, saying that he promised to take her: when she was ninety, she could ask him again and they would go. Laura died and on many occasions he felt remorse for not having gratified that wish, for not having realized that her situation was so serious. After her mother's death Caroline went to live with Divina. She was José Flávio's youngest sister, who was very fond of her niece. She had four children of her own, two of whom were girls aged three and five. One afternoon, some years after Laura's death, José Flávio went to his sister's house, as he normally did after leaving the office, and stayed there to drink coffee and talk with Divina and his brother-in-law. They were talking about Sr. Lionel, an old man of eighty-four who had decided to sell his ranch. Nobody could believe it. When he went to the courthouse and signed over the deed, many people gathered at the door to convince themselves that it was really the truth.

"He must be going soft in the head," Divina commented.

José Flávio didn't agree and she said, "Then why did he agree to this proposal now, if earlier he wouldn't sell for any price?"

"I don't know, but he isn't going soft in the head. He must have had some good reason." He added, "I have no doubt."

The brother-in-law agreed that the old man was quite lucid.

"More brains than any of us."

They talked about this, and when he left, Caroline followed him to the car. He had gotten a dustpan and a small plastic bag from the kitchen to clean out the grains of rice that had spilled in the trunk, and she went with him. José Flávio bent over with his head inside the trunk and she stayed there beside him, waiting for him to finish cleaning up the rice.

"Daddy," she said, "I want to live with you."

Surprised, José Flávio raised his head and looked at her.

"I want to go to my house," she continued.

"But your house is here, daughter," he replied. He wanted to know, "Has anything happened?"

"No, I just want to live with you." She added, "My house isn't here, it's where you live."

José Flávio didn't know how to answer her. He asked, "Don't you like living here with your aunt?"

"Yes, Daddy, but I want to live in my house."

He looked at her attentively. Perhaps it was the first time he had really taken a good look at this eight-year-old daughter of his: a quiet little girl with large eyes, neither happy nor sad, delicate but showing a firmness that surprised him. In his sister's house she was treated exactly like the other children. Seeing her in their midst, no one could say which were his sister's own and which was the niece. He had never heard any complaint whatsoever about anything his sister did. José Flávio thought about this, watching Caroline standing before him with her big black eyes, just like Laura's. Her hair was the same, too: the color was identical, the same soft waves.

She was a pretty child, and he told her, "Take this dustpan and the plastic bag to the kitchen. When I come back tomorrow we'll talk about this some more."

"All right," she answered.

They exchanged kisses and he got in the car and drove off, trying to imagine why she had come up with that idea. He wondered if his sister, brother-in-law, or their children could have done or said something, but he ruled that possibility out. Divina and her husband really did treat Caroline like a daughter and all her cousins loved her. And nobody had ever made any suggestion or dropped any hint that she should come back to stay with him. The fact of her living at Divina's house was seen as something natural. He had no wife, his daughter lived with one of his sisters. Everyone understood. Even Laura's parents, when they came to see Caroline, showed no surprise that she was living with Divina.

The next day when José Flávio stopped by his sister's

house, he acted the same as usual. He chatted, had a cup of coffee. When he was leaving, his daughter went outside with him.

"I've been thinking about what you said to me yesterday. You see, at my house there's no one but Tanise," he said, referring to the maid. "I only come home for lunch and to sleep." He asked her who would keep her company, who she would play with.

"There's my friends at school," she answered. "And besides, I can come here to Aunt Divina's house and play whenever I want."

For a moment he looked at her in silence. Then he said, "We'll talk some more tomorrow."

That evening he exchanged ideas with Thelma, a girl he was dating.

"Never in these four years have I noticed any sign of maladjustment. She's a child who doesn't miss people much or get too attached to them."

He spoke to his girlfriend as if he were thinking out loud, trying to find some explanation of his daughter's wish. Thelma was intelligent and thought it was normal that Caroline would want to live with him, but José Flávio could tell that deep down she didn't like the idea. He asked his parents' advice, too. He went to see them early one morning before going to the office. When he arrived, his mother was still in bed. His father, who rose earlier, often went to the market to buy fish, then to the bakery for bread. By the time he got back José Flávio's mother would be up and they would have breakfast. José Flávio went into the bedroom in which the curtains were still drawn, sat down on the bed, and conversed. His mother talked about his brothers and sisters, the grandchildren, and when his father came in and opened the curtains, José Flávio said that he was thinking about taking Caroline back to live with him. His mother thought that the little girl would limit him somewhat and would also be a worry.

"Has something happened?" she asked.

José Flávio replied that nothing whatever had happened.

"Have you talked to Caroline to see what she thinks of this?" his father wanted to know.

"It was her idea. She came and asked me."

"It's just a childish whim. In a few days she'll forget the whole thing, you'll see," his father concluded.

His mother agreed. "Before long she'll forget."

Then José Flávio talked to Divina and his brother-in-law. He could see the tears filling his sister's eyes.

"The decision is yours and Caroline's. Whatever you decide I'll have to accept," Divina told him, after saying many things in praise of her niece.

When he went out, José Flávio called his daughter.

"I've thought some more, and if it's what you want, then we'll live together," he said. They were at the gate of the house, beside the car, and she opened her arms, embraced him, and kissed him several times.

"Right away she'll start to miss the other children and want to come back," the aunts and uncles predicted.

On the day of the move Caroline went to school in the morning, and Divina took her clothes to José Flávio's house. She arranged them in the wardrobe and gave Tanise directions, explaining what Caroline like to eat, what she had for breakfast, what she took to school for a snack. She warned the maid that she would have to remind Caroline to brush her teeth at night and, when she came out of the bath, see that her ears had been washed properly. And if she should start to cough after being out in the cold, Tanise was to take a handkerchief moistened in alcohol and tie it around her neck when she went to bed.

"Then she'll wake up feeling fine."

At first, Caroline sometimes called José Flávio "uncle," but after a few days she stopped confusing him with Divina's husband. She and her father had breakfast together, then he dropped her off at school and went to the office. They had lunch together, too. At first he listened with a certain impatience to her tales, to the things she had learned in school, the games with her classmates. She spoke very slowly and he had to control himself so as not to keep telling her to eat.

It was an effort not to say, "Finish your yogurt," or "Drink your juice." "You've hardly eaten anything and it's time to go."

Little by little he grew accustomed to her pace of speaking and eating and saw that she always finished in time to leave without making him late. Once, at lunch, he was preoccupied with some rice buyers who were coming to meet him that afternoon, and when he looked at Caroline's face, he saw that she was crying. She was eating her food with tears running down her face.

"What's wrong?" he asked.

She didn't answer, just kept on crying silently. That night when he came home, he saw that she was all right. He found her standing on a chair playing with a puppet. It was a wooden duck connected by wires to two crossed sticks that she commanded, making the duck move its feet, its neck, its head. She made it walk, peck at a grain of corn, and drink water from a cup. Her expression was normal as she talked with him, but she didn't tell him why she had cried at lunchtime. He didn't ask and she didn't volunteer any reason. They left the subject alone.

Thelma became friends with Caroline. At first she wanted to treat her like a daughter, trying to give her advice, teach her things. But Caroline would talk about her school, her classmates, her cousins, would show Thelma her notebooks and act as if they were merely friends. Once the two of them were in the bedroom talking and José Flávio heard Caroline refer to Laura. She was saying that her mother had died because she was sick a long time.

"She would lie there with her face to the wall, not wanting to talk to anyone," she said.

She had always been tired and had to take medicine. The night table was full of bottles of medicine, but they hadn't helped, she died all the same.

"Daddy bought her so much medicine but she didn't get well," explained the girl.

Caroline and José Flávio had breakfast together and went out together, but she got up fifteen minutes earlier because she took longer to get ready. The alarm clock was at her bedside, and after she woke up, she would kneel to say her prayers, which she liked to do in the morning instead of at night. She prayed to God and Our Lady for her mother up in heaven, for her father, her grandparents, aunts, uncles, and cousins. She prayed that she would be a good girl. Then she said the Lord's Prayer, got up, opened the curtains, changed the date on the calendar that sat on her desk, went to the wall, and crossed off the previous day on another calendar that hung there. And then she would go into the bathroom. She did everything extremely calmly and methodically, and only when she came out of the bathroom did she go past the door of her father's room, which was always half-open, and call to him. One day she called him earlier than usual.

"Daddy, oh Daddy," she cried. Then she said something he didn't catch.

"What is it?"

"There's an animal in the bathroom."

"An animal?" he asked, still half-asleep.

"Yes, Daddy. A rat. It's in the toilet."

José Flávio got up, went to the bathroom, and sure enough, inside the toilet was a large gray rat, its hind feet resting on the bottom of the toilet. With its front feet against the side, it kept its head and part of its body above water. Its whiskers were clearly visible as it peered out, and its beady eyes shone.

Caroline was standing at the door and José Flávio told her, "Use the other bathroom."

Then he went to the kitchen, got a broom, and hit the rat on the head several times, drowning it in the toilet—a highly disagreeable process. When it was dead, he fished it out, wrapped it in newspaper, and told Tanise to throw it in the trash. He sat down at the breakfast table but couldn't manage to eat and only drank a cup of coffee.

"Did you get him out, Daddy?" Caroline asked.

"Yes, I did," said José Flávio.

"Did you kill him?"

"I killed him with a broom."

She went on eating naturally, and José Flávio tried not to show the sensation of disgust he felt. There was a moment of silence then she asked, "Daddy, why did he go inside the toilet?"

José Flávio explained that the rat had probably been thirsty and went after a drink of water.

"But how did he know there was water there?"

"From the smell."

"Can rats smell water?"

Yes, he confirmed, they could. Later, in the car, she asked how the rat had gotten into the house.

"Probably through the door or an open window."

"Did any more get in?"

"I don't know, sweetheart, but I don't think so."

He told her that in any case, it was a good idea for her always to look in the toilet first before she sat down. He asked her if the rat had startled her.

"Not exactly," she answered. "I was scared. I saw him there, looking at me, and it scared me." She agreed to do as her father suggested: always to look inside the toilet before sitting down. But no more rats appeared and she didn't mention the incident again.

Near them lived Bernardo, a city councilman who used to play soccer. He could kick so hard that when he took a free kick after a foul, the wall of players protecting the goal had to turn their backs to him. He was heavy, and he had to stop playing because twice in a row he fell down and fractured his left hand. The fingers couldn't support his weight when he tried to catch himself. Even after the cast came off, they still hurt and he had trouble moving his fingers. So he decided to quit playing soccer. When he was a boy, he lived on the ranch with his father, Sr. Diógenes, who planted cotton. When picking time came, he took his sons out of school to help him. Bernardo resented this and dreaded spending whole days in the hot sun, sweating, picking the white bolls of cotton from the stems, and putting them into a sack. All the children were paid for their work. In the afternoon, the cotton he and each of the brothers had picked was weighed, and they were paid according to the weight. Bernardo thought that was an absurd method of payment.

"Cotton doesn't weigh anything," he said.

Every year at cotton-picking time he would think about going away and leaving the farm. His mother's brother, Hilton, who owned a store in the city, had always treated him well when they went to visit, talking with Bernardo attentively. So when Bernardo finished the courses offered in the rural school, he asked his uncle if he could use someone to help him at the store.

"I want to go to the city to continue my studies," he said. The part about studying was a lie.

His uncle thought it was a good idea, but his parents didn't like it at all. Even so, Bernardo moved to town. He went to live with his uncle, working in the store during the day and studying at night. In the backyard there was a huge mango tree and a pigpen. His uncle took better care of the tree than of the pigs. Before Bernardo went to his classes, he had to gather the mangoes that had fallen to the ground, put them in a crate, and take them to the pigpen. His uncle would occasionally climb up to the top of the tree and prune the branches, correcting their growth, so that the tree flourished and spread until it was the biggest one in the city.

When there was talk of cutting it down to make an alley through the middle of their backyard, his uncle got very upset. He said he would never permit such a thing.

But Bernardo started to feel that his uncle was exploiting him, making him work too hard. They had an argument and he left his job, moved out of his uncle's house, and quit school. He went to live in a room behind a riverfront bar. The room had no lock, so inside he kept only a camp cot and a blanket. The place was full of mosquitoes and fleas. Bernardo stayed by the riverbank helping to load and unload boats. He remained there until his uncle invited him to come back to live with him again. The uncle arrived one day and talked to him. He said that they had argued and fought but that he should come back. He mentioned his wife and three daughters.

"Edith and the girls like you very much."

On the day they had argued, they were both nervous and had said things that weren't true.

"We should make peace, forget all that." He looked around the room and said that it wasn't right. The room was filthy and Bernardo was getting thinner.

"It isn't right for you to live so poorly if you're my nephew and I'm right here in the city."

So Bernardo went back to his uncle's house and Hilton himself found him a job working in a warehouse that handled bottled drinks.

"You don't have to work at my store, but stay at our house," he said.

Bernardo went back to school. Before long he got a better job at an oculist's shop, and as his finances improved he began to play soccer for his school team. One day he told his uncle that he wanted to pay him something for board and room.

The uncle didn't want to accept, but Bernardo said, "You never asked me to pay for anything, but now I'm able to, and I want you to take it."

It was to make him feel better, he explained. Later on he moved out of his uncle's house, took an exam for the Postal Service, married, got elected city councilman. Still he never neglected to visit his uncle. One day Hilton died of cancer, after only two months in bed. During those two months the disease wasted him down to skin and bones. Bernardo worried about him a great deal, but he couldn't see that Edith or the girls were very concerned. Even on the day of the funeral they didn't cry beside the casket. And they hadn't spent the night watching beside the body; they had stayed a few hours and left. Two daughters, who stayed the longest, went off in a corner and at times actually giggled. He was there to testify how his uncle had worked hard for his family.

Seeing him laid out, horribly thin, face covered with a veil and a crucifix in his hands, he said to himself, "It's an outrage. A good man who worked hard all his life for those women! To get this kind of a farewell!"

Even the casket was of inferior quality. After the funeral he couldn't contain himself; he spoke his mind to Edith and the daughters.

"If I hadn't watched through the night with him, he would have been all alone."

The whole thing made him very upset. At the first meeting of the City Council, he presented a project to declare the mango tree and part of his uncle's backyard public property. He justified the project with arguments for the tree's beauty and utility: its shade and fruit benefited everyone. Moreover, it was the biggest tree in the city and, as such, was a symbol to be preserved. Bernardo mobilized the schoolteachers and students, the ecologists, the lovers of nature. The city passed the law. And at the dedication ceremony Bernardo made a speech and put up a plaque on a cement pedestal next to the mango tree. On the plaque were written the legal articles that protected the tree from being cut down.

Next door to the house of Bernardo's uncle was the public jail, where a man called Ticiano spent several months in prison, waiting to be tried. He was the son of Sr. Norton, a dairy farmer who sold the milk produced by his seventy-eight cows to the cooperative called Producers Central. Ticiano would drive the milk to the co-op building every morning in his pickup truck. Then he formed a partnership with a fellow called Petrílio, and they bought a larger truck and began hauling milk for other farmers. They also bought butter and cheese from those who didn't belong to the cooperative. They bought and sold and their business grew until it became one of the largest dairy-handling operations in the region. Two other brothers, Caio and Décio, went into the same business as competitors, offering better prices, taking away old customers, and making trouble for Ticiano's firm. One day Ticiano happened upon them in a roadside bar near a gas station and accused them of stealing from him. There was an argument, and Ticiano ended up pulling out a revolver and killing them both. It was late at night and chaos ensued. This wasn't the first time Ticiano had gotten into an argument and shot someone. Once he fired at the owner of a little store, accusing him of cheating on the price of some cans of kerosene. But he missed, so he didn't go to prison. With the death of his brothers Caio and Décio, he was sent straight to jail and stayed there while the case came to trial. Petrílio, his partner, occasionally needed him to sign business papers. Soon the warden began to permit Ticiano to go to the firm's office accompanied by a guard. But before very long Ticiano began to argue with his partner, too, saying that he was doing business on his own, ignoring their agreement.

"Just because I'm in jail, eh?" he said, "Well, remember that I may be in jail, but I'm not blind!"

The warden learned of the arguments and suspended Ticiano's privilege of going out. Petrílio had to send someone to the jail with the papers that needed signing. Many of them Ticiano refused to sign. He would read them, reread them, and start to swear, saying that his partner was cheating him.

The warden heard him say that Petrílio should be killed, too, and commented, "You're already in prison for murder, and you still want to kill people?"

"What can I do, Warden? Everybody's a thief!"

Near the jail was Boa Vista Street, where Aluísio lived. He was married to Vanessa and they had six children. He bought and sold construction materials and liked to raise pigs. He dealt in cement, bricks, and wood. When an opportunity arose for him to represent a company that sold caustic lime, he accepted the proposition. He received loads of lime, sifted out the impurities, distributed it into sacks, and sold it. He and Vanessa, in spite of their many children, led a fairly easy life. They had their house, the depository for construction materials, and a small plot of land where Aluísio raised his pigs. But after he became the lime company's representative things went even better. He started earning lots of money. He enlarged and redecorated his house, bought a truck, made the depository bigger, and started something you really could call a pig-raising operation.

Vanessa was the daughter of Proença, a boatman who had been terrible at managing money. Her strongest childhood memories were of her mother, Dona Lenira, praying on her knees every night with her children, begging Our Lady to deliver their father from the dangers of the river and help him pay his debts. She was always warning her children not to spend money, to economize.

"Your father has many debts to pay," she would say to the children.

If he didn't pay them, the creditors would take away everything they possessed, "And we'll have to live off other people's charity," she explained.

Vanessa spent her childhood in great fear of penury and homelessness, of being obliged to carry her belongings around in a suitcase, dependent on some relative's charity. When she and Aluísio became sweethearts, she decided to marry him because he transmitted to her the impression that life was not so dramatic or serious. He inspired confidence. At his side she felt secure and unafraid. Though he worked hard, it didn't seem difficult for him to get things.

Evanildes, their oldest daughter, often complained as she grew bigger, "Mother, this is ridiculous, Dad filling up the living room with these pictures."

And she would point to the photographs, all of which showed Aluísio near a very large or very fat pig. Or bending over a sow surrounded by piglets.

"I don't know how you can stand it, Mother."

Vanessa at times really did find it strange, but she accepted the pictures with no real difficulty.

"He enjoys the pigs," she would answer. "What's wrong with that?"

"Nobody has photos of pigs on their living-room wall, Mother. Nobody but us."

Vanessa accepted the photos and many other things uncomplainingly. She accepted the business meetings at night, the unexpected trips, the weekends at the farm with Aluísio thinking only of the pigs.

"The main thing is, I feel secure," she would confess to herself.

When she considered the possibility of her husband meeting other women, she would rationalize, "Well, we have six kids to raise, so what are a few annoyances?"

Aluísio had always enjoyed playing cards, and after he started representing the lime company and always had plenty of money, he was sought out by his poker-playing friends. He became one of the group who always gambled and he started playing, and losing, regularly. With time he gambled more and lost more, and eventually he began to be late with his payments. His children's small requests annoyed him, and he complained of expenses. Then he sold his car and truck and bought a used pickup. He didn't tell Vanessa anything about his business, but she could see that things weren't going so well. And she changed, too. She became insecure and they started to have misunderstandings, then fights. She no longer accepted all his views as she had before and began to demand that he come home earlier, that he tell her where he had been and with whom. She nagged and belittled him in front of the children. The peace she had felt at his side disappeared and her old childhood fear and insecurity came back. Any small thing could start her cursing at him; she had no self-control. On the weekends his gambling friends would come to get him and he hardly took care of the pigs anymore. He didn't even go to the farm. Vanessa started to do what she had always condemned in her mother: to call her children together, kneel with them, and pray that Our Lady would deliver them from poverty so they wouldn't be forced to live off other people's charity.

One day Aluísio drove the pickup truck into a tree and came home with his forehead bruised. He said that the sun had gotten into his eyes.

"I looked at the sun and couldn't see anything."

From then on, his eyes watered constantly and he couldn't keep them open for very long at a time. He went to an eye doctor and learned that the cause of his trouble was the caustic lime he sifted in the depository. He didn't wear goggles, and the lime was burning his eyes. Moreover, it was too late to prevent him going blind. Vanessa's reaction to this terrible situation was impressive. She showed great dedication to her husband and did everything to help him. Even with the six children, three of whom were still small, she would drive him to the construction warehouse and stay there at his side. Aluísio gave her instructions as to how each problem should be resolved and she made things run, following his orders to the letter and informing her husband as to what wasn't going right. Even the pigs were once again taken care of properly. The two would go to the farm, he would ask questions and give orders to the workers. She would observe, describing everything she saw. The friction and arguments ceased, and Vanessa once again felt secure and confident in Aluísio's company. But the waters came and covered their house, the pig farm, the construction warehouse, and also the home of a woman called Sinara.

Sinara had been widowed at age thirty-five. When she was forty-eight, she met Robson, the man she lived with. He was eleven years younger than Sinara. He worked in a butcher shop and, before meeting her, had already walked past her house admiring the size of the backyard, because he had always wanted to raise quails and guans, and in Sinara's yard there was plenty of space for that. He had been married to Hortensia, a nervous woman who was forever complaining about how he smelled when he got home. At that time he worked in a tannery and the strong odor of the solution in which they immersed the hides clung to him. Hortensia could never get used to it. After one of their fights he decided to break up with her, because he was already displeased with her interest in Sr. Euler, the owner of the bar. So they parted ways. Just as he suspected, Hortensia at once went to work for Sr. Euler, who enlarged his saloon, put in three pool tables and two tabletop soccer games, the kind with the players on handles. Hortensia was hired to supervise, serve drinks, and sell betting chips. The bar grew much more lively. At night it was always full of young men conversing, playing cards, drinking, and looking at his ex-wife's rear end, shown off now in short, tight skirts. She seemed very pleased with herself. Robson couldn't have cared less. He left the tannery and went to work for the Trustworthy butcher shop, where in a short time he came to know all the customers by name. He kept his eye on Sinara after he saw her house with its spacious backyard. He would choose the best pieces of meat, cut them carefully, and wrap them up, all ready for her to collect. Some people didn't speak too kindly about his intentions, but that didn't bother him. He made his conquest and moved in with Sinara. Her children didn't like to see him living with their mother and Robson didn't let that bother him either. He had a plan to raise quails and guans, and he wanted to put it into practice. He did a few experiments and found that the best birds were a variety called "Japanese," which were smaller and laid better than the others. They were smarter, too, eating and running as soon as they hatched. When he came home from the butcher shop in the afternoon, he spent the rest of the day in the backyard, taking care of the poultry. He treated Sinara with consideration and respect and didn't interfere in her children's business. The children were grown up and married, and when they came to visit her, they talked and argued a lot.

He used bantam hens to hatch the quail eggs, as a friend from the tannery had taught him. When the little quails hatched, he put them into crates with light bulbs burning inside. When they were thirty days old, he separated the males from the females. The males fought constantly when they were together and often got hurt. He planted a bed of collard greens to feed them and felt very pleased with his project. The guans were less work. The hens took care of their own nests and they didn't need special feed. They would eat anything. They cleaned the ground of insects, fruit peels, and seeds. Whatever they found, they swallowed. The only thing to remember was that you couldn't have a tree in the area where they were kept, because they could easily get up into the branches and go flying away. Apart from this, they gave him no work or worry. But hardly anyone was interested in buying them. Even the eggs sold poorly. The quails, on the other hand, sold well—even the young roosters, the older hens, the eggs, everything.

When he had nine hundred quails and one hundred and ten guans, Robson did some calculations and quit his job at the butcher shop. That was when he and Sinara began to quarrel, due to her children's constant complaints about his living there. She started to find fault with everything. Robson just kept his mouth shut. He didn't answer because he had all those quails and guans and he thought to himself, If we break up and she puts me out in the street, what will I do with all these birds?

He had also begun crossing guans with Asiatic chickens and was getting vigorous, nice-looking fighting cocks. Interested people were already coming to see and buy the crossbred birds. Sinara's children kept criticizing and cursing him because he spent the day in the backyard and didn't work in the butcher shop anymore. Sinara, influenced by what they said, began to complain. He didn't argue. It was her house and he had nowhere to go with his poultry. He continued to accept her intolerance, taking care of his birds and doing the things she wanted him to, like cutting down the grass around the fences or fixing the broken furniture and faulty electric plugs. But it was no use. The third time she told him to get out, he began to sell all his quails and guans. He sold them all, took down the nests, dismantled the crates for the chicks, and left the house without argument or discussion. He went back to the tannery, making plans and promising himself that one day he would have a piece of ground. He would marry a younger woman who could help him, and dedicate himself to raising birds, which he had learned to do successfully.

On the street where Sinara lived were two houses built close to one another, where a father and his son lived. The first one belonged to Sr. Gustavo and Dona Rosali and the second to their only son, Paulo Roberto, who was married to Gislene. She was always suspicious of him around other women. She was so jealous that she even complained to her mother-in-law, who in the evening would say to Gustavo, "Gislene came over complaining about Paulo Roberto again."

"What is it this time?"

"She said he was in the door of the Pearl dry-goods store holding some girl's hand. Another of her silly stories," Dona Rosali remarked.

"What do you mean, stories? He probably was holding some girl's hand," Gustavo answered.

It was always that way between them. Dona Rosali thought her daughter-in-law's suspicions were exaggerated and Gustavo affirmed that there was no straightening out the son.

"When *wasn't* he after some girl?" he would ask.

Ever since he was little, Paulo Roberto had caused problems with his girl chasing. When the boy was five, a neighbor had asked Sr. Gustavo to have a talk with him.

"He's annoying Dione," the neighbor said, referring to his three-year-old daughter.

"Annoying, how?" Gustavo wanted to know.

The neighbor explained that Paulo Roberto couldn't set eyes on his daughter without wanting to grab her hand and take her underneath the staircase. He had asked the girl, "Dione, tell Daddy where Paulo takes you."

"Under the stairs."

"And when you get there, what does he do?"

"Takes my panties off."

"And what else?"

"He grabs my bottom."

"And does he want to do other things?"

"Yes, stick his wee-wee in my wee-wee."

"Just his wee-wee?"

"No, his finger, too."

"This is turning into a problem," the neighbor said to Gustavo.

Rosali couldn't leave the boy alone a minute, for Paulo Roberto would be trying to get Dione under the stairs. Problems were always coming up. The children on that street wanted to have parties when they were eight or nine. He was the most enthusiastic. He would ask his mother to buy soda pop, make cookies and snacks while he chose the music and made a list of the girls to be invited. At every party he organized, the lights would go out from time to time. One day Gustavo overheard him talking to a classmate. The boys were in Paulo Roberto's bedroom.

"They might not like it," the boy said, disagreeing with some idea.

"All right, you just kiss them, then," Paulo Roberto answered.

The two were planning their strategy. One of them,

after choosing the girl, would give a signal by scratching his head. The other would go to the fuse box and turn off all the lights. The classmate preferred to turn them off in the intervals between records because, if the girl was dancing at the time, he wouldn't know where her mouth was.

"I can't hit the mark," he explained.

"Fine," Paulo Roberto agreed. And he said, "But when I give the signal, don't turn the lights back on until the girls start to scream."

Paulo Roberto took advantage of the darkness not only to kiss the girls, but also to put his hand up their skirts. When Gustavo reminded his wife of these things, Rosali would defend their son.

"It was the girls' fault. They made him act like that, showing themselves off in those short dresses."

Paulo Roberto had two scars on his left leg, marks made by a fish hook meant for catching dorado or other big fish. The hooks had been embedded so deeply that they had taken him to the hospital to get them out. He was ten at the time, and had heard that certain girls sunbathed nude on the rocks near the canal. In this part of the river, rows of isolated rocks extended out into midstream, forming a sort of arm. Here the current flowed very quickly, beating against these rocks, and it was common for fishermen to leave baited hooks in the water. Hardly anyone ventured to swim there, but at times people hopped from rock to rock and sunbathed there, invisible from the bank. Someone told Paulo Roberto that when the girls went there alone, they would take off their bathing suits to tan all over. The person even told him some of the girls' names and Paulo Roberto went there to wait. He saw three of them jump from rock to rock until they were out of sight of the bank, and he decided to follow them. Worried that they would see him approaching, he went the most dangerous way. He slipped, fell into the current, got tangled in the fish lines, and was cut by the hooks. He grabbed onto an outcropping of rock, bleeding and screaming for help. His friends, seeing him from the bank, gave the alarm and some men hurried out to rescue him.

Paulo Roberto created these and many other problems due to his mania for chasing women. He made holes in the bathroom door to spy on his cousins. He forced his way into the maids' room when they were asleep. On the sly, he kissed his girlfriends' sisters. Even so, Rosali defended her son, always saying that Gislene was far too jealous.

Gustavo, referring to his daughter-in-law, would comment, "I certainly feel sorry for that girl."

Near them, a few doors down, had lived a man called Sinval, who made furniture. He liked to listen to music and go fishing on weekends. He was careful and meticulous in his work and considerate of other people. He had two children, and one Saturday, four days after he turned twenty-nine, he died of a cerebral aneurysm. On the morning of his death he went to the house of a friend called Otomar, who was sitting on the veranda drinking beer with his brothers-in-law. Sinval joined them, had a beer, and he and Otomar made plans to go fishing the next day, a Sunday. They chatted and told jokes. Otomar was good at telling jokes, and Sinval laughed a lot. At one point he stopped laughing and put his hand to his head.

"What is it?" asked Otomar.

"I heard a sort of noise inside here," answered Sinval.

The others looked at him, worried.

"It's nothing," he said, and started laughing again.

"Probably your head can't take any more of Otomar's filthy jokes," one of the brothers-in-law said, chuckling.

"That must be it," joined in Sinval.

They kept on talking and laughing until Cirlene, Sinval's wife, came to pick him up. They had planned for her to come get him at lunchtime. He always preferred to drive when they went anywhere together by car, but this time, without a word, he got in and sat down on the passenger's side, which made Cirlene suspect that something wasn't quite right. When they got home, the maid served lunch, but he didn't eat. He sat down, but got up at once to take something for his headache. Then he went into the bathroom.

"I'm feeling sort of nauseous," he said.

Cirlene went on eating lunch with the children. Sinval took a long time coming back, and finally she went to see if he needed anything. She found him crumpled on the floor, unconscious and breathing with difficulty. She screamed for the neighbor, and they took him to the hospital, but he never came out of it. He never regained consciousness, and he died that night. It was a cerebral aneurysm, the doctors explained. Everyone in the family had heard of people who died of aneurysms or strokes, but never their relatives or anyone very close.

"It was a lesion in one of the cerebral veins. Then the vein can dilate and break," the doctors said.

Maybe he had been born with it, or it could have been caused by something else, like a blow on the head, for example. It was hard, almost impossible, to determine if the vein would burst, let alone when. They all were shocked by Sinval's death, and as they listened to the doctors' explanations, Eugênia, his mother, who was a well-preserved woman and still pretty at fifty-four, looked at Josué, her oldest son. He was five years older than Sinval and his eyes were still swollen from crying and lack of sleep. He was listening attentively to the doctors and Eugênia knew exactly what he was thinking at that moment.

A few days later, when she heard him refer to the time he had made Sinval fall and hit his head, she answered, "I don't remember, son. I think you must be mixed up."

But she did remember. Sinval standing in the cradle, struggling but unable to get over the railing. Josué coming in with a horse's halter in his hand. She herself immediately hearing the terrible thump, running to find Josué still holding the end of the halter rope in his hand, the halter he had thrown over Sinval's head. She could still see Sinval unconscious on the floor. She carried him to her bedroom, calling to him, but he didn't answer. She remembered placing a cold knife against the bump that was swelling high on his forehead, throwing water in his face. Very slowly, little by little, he regained consciousness. When her husband came home, the two kept talking with him, not letting him go to sleep for fear he wouldn't wake up again. Sinval was less than a year old, but from then on, he was never the same as before. From her experience with her older children she knew for certain that he was different. Calmer, more resigned. If he hadn't had that head injury, he would have been happier, more expansive. He had lost the energy that he had shown in the first few months of his life.

"Children play, and do things they shouldn't," she said

to herself after his death. "But why did Josué have to throw a halter over his brother's head and pull him out of the cradle?"

She thought about this and was afraid that Josué or one of her other children might read her thoughts. She claimed she couldn't remember the incident, but she remembered perfectly the thudding noise of Sinval's head against the floor. And then his headaches, the sudden blockings of his larynx when he was asleep, for which the doctors could find no cause. His nightmares about being suffocated, and his wakening to run to the window, opening it in his anxiety to fill his lungs with air. His growing up different from the others, having these problems and maybe for that very reason becoming more attached to her. Many times he was the only one to know of her worries and fears. She thought about this, and when the other children, principally Josué, would come up and start to talk about Sinval, she would change the subject, afraid that they would read her thoughts.

Sinval lived on this street, Sinval who died of a cerebral aneurysm at age twenty-nine, and Dona Sinara, the widow who lived for a while with Robson and his quails and guans. Also Paulo Roberto the womanizer and his wife, Gislene. This street ran perpendicular to Belmont Street, which at its lower end was crossed by a small stream of water called Calf Creek. Sometimes the creek would swell a little during the rainy season, but it never got higher than the backyards of a few houses, like that belonging to Mabel, a young woman who served hot meals for a living and, when she married at age seventeen, tried to stay away from pasta, bread, and desserts because she was afraid of getting too plump, though her husband, Everardo, declared she had the most gorgeous body in the world.

Their marriage lasted. "Seven years, four months and eleven days," she would say with her eyes brimming, whenever she referred to Everardo's death.

Even after the worst phase was over, her tears still flowed when his name was spoken. He had been an agronomist and left her with three children, a house in the city, and a ranch, which she sold in order to cancel the debts that Everardo had contracted precisely in order to buy it. Besides the need to pay off the debts, she sold the ranch because she couldn't stand to go back there. She couldn't bear to go into the room where he had fallen and she, at the crucial moment, had dodged away, then turned back to see him collapsed on the floor. She had taken his head onto her lap as the blood seeped onto her dress and hands.

She had screamed, "Everardo! Everardo!"

But he was already gone. And she couldn't stop blaming herself for not trying to break his fall.

"If he had fallen onto me, he wouldn't have died," she repeated, as if obsessed.

The money that had been left over after the debt was paid off wasn't much, and her family and Everardo's helped her out. They were not wealthy families, but they started to present her with clothes, shoes, and baskets of food.

"I can't do it," she would say, thinking of facing life without her husband.

With three children, her burden of guilt, and no education (for she had never studied or worked outside the home) the problems seemed insoluble to her. She had no energy to do anything, not even to take care of herself and the children. At times she didn't even want to get out of bed.

"Mabel, you have to get hold of yourself," her relatives all told her. She knew she needed to get hold of herself, but how? Where could she find strength? So she did nothing, and the hours and days passed in painful slowness. There was a period when she overate, trying to escape her memories of Everardo falling off the ladder. She would get out of bed, go to the kitchen, and devour everything in sight, trying to forget the last weekend they had spent together on the ranch.

"Mabel, you're gaining weight, you need to take control of yourself and the children. Look how they run around," her mother and sisters would say. But she continued to stay in bed, only getting up to go to the kitchen and eat whatever she found there. She remembered Everardo getting the ladder out of the chicken house to change the ceiling bulb in the living room. It was an old ladder that opened and closed, and its metal joints were rusty.

As she watched him climb up she had told him, "This ladder is going to fall apart."

Everardo wasn't paying any attention and she repeated, "This ladder's ready to fall apart, it's so old."

He climbed up and she stayed beneath to help him. Everardo unscrewed the burnt-out light bulb and leaned over to give it to her in exchange for the new one. As he straightened up again, stretching to reach the socket, one of the ladder's legs escaped from its hinge. Mabel dodged involuntarily as the ladder came apart and saw her husband fall onto his back. She quickly took his head in her lap and called to him, even screamed, but he was already dead.

Mabel couldn't get away from these memories. One day she was in her room, lying down as usual, when she heard her brother yelling at her children to take their hands out of the basket. He must be arriving with supplies of food and the children probably wanted to grab something. Mabel's brother scolded them as if he were scolding a dog.

"Get away from there, get your hands off!" he screamed at Elísio, the oldest. He screamed at the others, too, and slapped Regis, who was four. Mabel heard the blow and her son's crying. It was from that day on that she started to recover. Her brother went away without coming to her room, without even speaking to her. He walked in, put the basket on the table, screamed at the children like you would at a dog, slapped Regis, and left. Mabel got up, went to the living room, and sat on a chair. She called her three children and asked them what had happened. Listening to their complaints, she saw how dirty and unkempt they were.

Then she got up, put the things from the basket into the cupboard, and said, "I'm going to give all of you a bath. Everyone into the bathroom."

She helped Helder, the littlest, to get his clothes off, and scrubbed and rinsed all three. From that moment things started to change. Although she knew her situation was very hard, she began to take action.

"I have to stand on my own two feet," she would say when her memories and feelings of guilt discouraged her, tempting her to lie prostrate in bed.

All she knew how to do was cook, so she concentrated her efforts on cooking to make money. She spread word among her neighbors, relatives, and acquaintances who owned shops that she was serving hot meals at her house. Customers began to appear, and she invested some of her savings in kitchen equipment. She served lunch and dinner at home and furnished hot meals for delivery. As time passed she came to have so many customers that people sometimes had to wait more than twenty minutes to be served. Her mother and father suggested that she try some other kind of activity.

"You're clever, why don't you learn sewing and work as a seamstress?"

They didn't think it was really appropriate for their daughter to turn her house into a restaurant. But she went right ahead. When she could no longer manage to do everything alone, she hired cooks and supervised them, working alongside them to make sure things were done correctly. She worked hard at her business, taking care of her house and children at the same time. She kept them clean, taught them things, showed them how to get along.

When she was afraid she couldn't manage alone, she would say to herself, "I may wear myself out, but I'll never let them be treated like dogs again."

On Belmont Street, where Mabel lived, there was a square with a church, Santa Rita Church. When it was being remodeled, a man called Filadelfo did the painting inside, which took a long time. He and a helper painted the walls of the nave, listening to Father Newton talk about his chickens. The parochial house was near the church and every morning and afternoon Father Newton would come by to see how the painting was going. And he never stopped talking about the chickens. They weren't good layers, but were wonderful for eating: large and fat, with small wings.

"Almost no unnecessary appendages," the priest would say. "Just the body with tender meat."

For several years he had been crossbreeding them, trying to get them to have smaller and smaller wings.

"A special breed," he confided to Filadelfo.

Filadelfo listened in silence and, when he quit work, would walk past the parochial residence, thinking about the big, almost-wingless chickens heavy with tender meat. Late one night, he returned to the street where the priest lived and entered the backyard. Even in the dark he didn't make a mistake, he knew his way by heart from having walked by there so often, studying the house and surrounding area. He jumped over the wall at one side and opened the chicken coop, but before he could get his hands on a hen, a dog bounded out, barking loudly. The priest woke up, turned on the light, and opened the bedroom window. Filadelfo barely had time to grab a young black and white rooster.

"If there aren't any wingless hens handy, you'll have to do," he said.

So he ate the rooster. Father Newton continued to stop by the church to inspect the paint job and he mentioned the thief that had broken into his chicken coop. Filadelfo listened in silence.

"This is the first time it's ever happened," said the priest. No one had ever entered his backyard before. If he hadn't heard the dog barking, turned on the light, and opened the window, the thief would have stolen his prize chickens. The priest put his hands behind his back and walked up and down as Filadelfo, up on the scaffolds, went on painting the wall and listening.

"Mind you, I don't talk to just anyone about my chickens."

Recently, in fact, he had only mentioned them there in the church. "Perhaps you noticed somebody hanging around who might be interested in my chickens?"

"No, Father, I haven't seen or heard anything," Filadelfo answered. "I'll be on the lookout to see if I can discover anything. But that will be hard because in this world there are many dishonest people, people who do things nobody would imagine. . . ."

The next morning the priest spoke of the great error that people committed in not following the commandments of God and of the Church. In not fulfilling their religious obligations. And he wanted to know when Filadelfo had last been to confession.

"It's been quite a while, Father."

Father Newton commented that among the religious obligations a person had, one of the most important was confession. To remain with sin on one's conscience was not a good thing. "To hide one's errors is to walk down the road to perdition."

"You're right, Father," Filadelfo said in answer. "Whoever has sinned ought to confess."

The priest said that many didn't fulfill their obligations to the Church because of lack of opportunity or even because of forgetfulness, and even mentioned that he was always at the disposal of his congregation.

"I'm here for anyone, at any time, to listen and pardon the faults they have committed."

Atop his ladder Filadelfo listened and pretended not to understand. After the priest left, he muttered between his teeth, "You want to find out who ate your rooster, Father? Well, don't hold your breath, because you won't find out from me."

Leonardo lived in the first house after the church. He was a surveyor whose face still carried the scars from chicken pox he had had when he was very small. He wasn't even big enough to crawl. His older brother, Hudson, went to visit their grandparents in a city farther away from the bank of the river and came back with signs of the disease. But their mother didn't keep the two brothers apart, having been taught that the younger ran no risk of getting chicken pox since breast-feeding made him immune. But he came down with such a severe case of the disease that they actually thought he might die.

"His little body is raw, poor thing," the mother said.

She remembered that at the time, she prayed constantly to the Holy Virgin to spare his life. He lived, but his face remained pockmarked. The small round scars covered not only his face but his neck and arms as well. He was married to Almira and the grassy lawn beside this house was decorated with a large section of eucalyptus trunk. Leonardo liked to relax there in the afternoon when he was finished measuring land. He would sit down, have a beer, and talk with friends who passed by and stopped for a chat, occasionally joining him in a glass. Every afternoon he could be found there in his shirt sleeves, having his drink and talking.

If one of his friends accepted a beer, he would turn and shout in his strong voice, "Almira, bring another glass!"

Hudson, the brother from whom he caught the chicken pox, had gone into the Merchant Marine and only come home twice since. Leonardo liked to repeat what his brother had told him about the customs of countries he had visited. For example, in some parts of India, when people were expecting visitors or giving a party, they would line the paths with candles in colored saucers and also put small vases of flowers on the ground. In the interior of Iraq they didn't use spoons and forks to eat. Everyone took his food from the same dish and ate it with his fingers—not only in homes, but in bars and restaurants, too. Leonardo liked to describe such customs that his brother had told him about. On weekends he liked to go fishing. He would tie down everything inside the boat, because once it had overturned. He and the friend who was with him had lost everything. Leonardo had hooked a seventy-pound dorado. As soon as the fish bit, he could tell it was a dorado and calculated its weight.

"Seventy pounds at least," he said to his friend.

This was around eleven o'clock at night, and the moon was full. He tried to tire the fish, playing out the line and reeling it in until at one point the dorado unexpectedly swam around behind the boat. Leonardo turned sharply but couldn't keep the boat facing the line, balanced against the dorado's pull. So the boat swamped. He and his friend fell into the water with all their clothes on. It was June, and Leonardo pulled off his sweater and jacket and the two shirts he was wearing on account of the cold. His friend got rid of all the extra clothes he could, too. They kept calm and didn't panic, because they knew that panic was what killed a lot of people. Then they righted the boat. While they were shedding clothes and getting the boat turned over, they saw the floater that was tied to the fish line bobbing off down the river, zigzagging, advancing, going back, until the fish grew tired and the floater stayed in one place near the bank. They got the boat right side up, rowed to where the floater was, and grabbed it. And they pulled that dorado out of the water. It was a seventy-pounder all right. They rowed back trembling with cold. The bottle of rum that the friend always took with him had disappeared in the water and they both caught bad colds. They had lost all their fishing gear—everything except an oar—but though they were shivering and wet, they were happy with the seventy-pound dorado shining in the bottom of the boat.

In this square near the Santa Rita Church and Leonardo's house there was a two-story building used as a student dormitory. Eight boys lived there, all sons of ranchers. One of them, whose name was Aécio, always got news from home. An employee of his father's would bring merchandise to the city twice a month and Adílio, his youngest brother, would send him long letters. So he always knew what was happening on the ranch even though he didn't go there. He knew why his father wanted to kill their dog, a bitch called Pirate. It was a Sunday and the father was sitting by the stove drinking okra broth in between sips of rum, which he liked to do before dinner. Amanda, the oldest sister, started to yell from the bank of the creek nearby. She had caught a fish that had escaped from the hook and was flopping around on the grass, trying to get back into the water again. The mother had just taken a roast chicken out of the oven and left it on the table as they went running out to see Amanda's fish—it was the first time she had ever caught anything. But the fish escaped and the father and mother went back laughing about all the confusion Amanda had caused. She didn't know what to do, just stood there shouting as she saw the trout work itself free of the hook, flip-flop on the ground, and fall back into the creek. Just as the father and mother were going into the house, they saw Pirate bounding out the kitchen door as fast as she could, carrying the chicken in her mouth. They all ran after her.

"Pirate, come back here!" the mother ordered.

But the bitch didn't stop. The father tripped over a rock and fell as he saw Pirate disappear into the woods, chicken and all.

"A roast chicken bigger than her head," Adílio had said in the letter.

The father was so angry that he loaded his shotgun and left it behind the kitchen door, waiting for Pirate to come back.

"But it seems she guessed. She won't come out of the woods when Dad is at home," wrote Adílio.

Aécio knew about the pair of blackbirds that made a nest in the orange tree in front of the living-room window. He knew when the mother bird laid the eggs, when the baby birds hatched, and when they learned to fly. Adílio wrote that the other bitch, Dolly, was much better. During his vacation she had lain down under the pickup and gotten run over accidentally. Dad hadn't seen her and had taken off in first gear, breaking all four of her legs. When vacation was over and Aécio went back to the city, Dolly couldn't even drag herself around. But Adílio sent news that she was recuperating. At first she couldn't move at all, then she could crawl over to get her food and water, and after a while, "She's up and walking around."

But she had to walk on only three legs. "The left hind leg went numb," Adílio wrote.

He told his brother about the peach trees and how many peaches were developing on the one beside the gate. They were still small, but tasty and sweet. He wrote when the mare Baroness had a bay male colt which everyone agreed would grow into a beautiful horse.

The mare Mulatinha was nearing her time to foal, too. Sired by Diplomat, the colt was born red but later turned chestnut. He wrote of the cow Beauty that was going dry; Dad was thinking of selling her to the butchers. Another cow, Polka Dot, had lost her calf. It was born too weak to survive. And he wrote when Darlene, their middle sister, started dating Ernani.

"The son of Sr. Rufino, who owns Challenger."

Challenger was a bull that had won two prizes at fairs. Darlene didn't leave the window, she was always waiting for Ernani to come along in his red-and-white pickup. Amanda warned her that she shouldn't let the boy know she cared so much about him, but Darlene paid no attention.

She stayed glued to the window, and when Amanda spoke to her about it again, she said, "I belong to the younger generation! I don't have the patience to listen to old people's ideas."

One of the letters told how they had discovered it was a lie that snakes, when they drank water, left their poison on the leaf of a plant and then got it back again. That same letter described Nino's birthday celebration. Nino was the head cowhand. He threw a party but even he didn't like the musicians he had found. There were three of them, very thin. Two played flutes and one a drum.

"They only knew music from their part of the country."

They were from Cachimbó and nobody knew their songs, which were no good to dance to either.

So Aécio studied in the city but kept in touch through his brother's letters with everything that happened back home. Next door to the dormitory where Aécio stayed lived Arlindo and Eulalia. Arlindo was the son of a very beautiful woman called Canuta. When he was three years old, she abandoned him. She went down the river with the campaign committee of some senator who was passing through in an elegant boat full of rich people, leaving Arlindo alone with his father Godofredo, who then started to drink. One day Godofredo found himself a skinny girl from the red-light zone and took her to live with him. And he sold the movie house to Sr. Clovis, the owner of the Metropolitan Bar. Clovis hired him to go on working as the projectionist. Although he was always drunk, Godofredo still managed to work. Later he died. Arlindo grew up hearing people talk about his mother, praising her beauty and spirit, and even her courage in leaving. Arlindo became an adult, married Eulalia, and they had two children, Maurícia and Sandro, and one afternoon they heard from his mother.

Thirty years ago she had gone down the river in the senator's boat and never sent a word of news, but now she announced, "I'm coming back."

The date of her arrival was set. Arlindo awaited her as one would a goddess. She came accompanied by a religious man, a preacher of some sort, a foreigner by the name of Parucker, who lavished attention on her. Elegant and sparkling with jewels, she talked a lot about the lands and riches she possessed. Arlindo and the children listened attentively and she gave her grandchildren toys and candy and spoke about the Bible. Maurícia started saying that when she grew up, she wanted to be like her grandmother Canuta. She would have jewels and many servants—one to comb her hair, another to massage her, another to take care of her dresses and shoes. Canuta got Arlindo to do whatever she wanted. She made him give money to Parucker and buy her a car to drive around while she was there. When she decided to leave town, she made him give up his job as warehouse manager of the Morais Brothers' Company and go down the river with her, leaving Eulalia and the children behind. They were to wait for him to come back to get them once he was established on his mother's property. But there were no lands or riches or maids. Canuta went down the river as she had done thirty years before, this time without the senator's committee but taking her son. Eulalia didn't hear from her husband for five months. She had to sell things from their house to support herself. She sold the furniture they had bought before her mother-in-law came and took in sewing until Arlindo came back. He was thin and worn out. The illusion he had had since childhood was undone now. Eulalia went to the office of old Sr. Morais, who didn't want to hire Arlindo back again, and sat in the waiting room for three hours. Three hours without leaving the place, accompanied by her children, tears streaming down her face. She explained to Sr. Morais everything that had happened and managed to convince him to rehire Arlindo. Then she forbade her children to speak the name of their grandmother, and forbade Maurícia to sleep hugging the Bible that Parucker had given her as a present.

From then on, whenever Arlindo made a decision that she didn't agree with, she would make him change his mind by saying, "Don't forget I sold the furniture out from under us to feed these children."

Across the square from them lived Ermínio, a lively man who from his youth had enjoyed parties and drinking with his friends. He dated several girls before he met Iraíldes and married her. He was twenty-seven when he really got to know her well. Before that, they had seen each other a few times but only from a distance. He was a commercial representative for various items, from plastic sandals and sewing thread to insecticides and sanitary products. Iraíldes taught history and geography in a Catholic parochial school. They started dating when two nieces of Ermínio took part in a sports tournament that was held every year among the schools of the city. The nieces, called Divana and Dinorah, were on the volleyball team. When they won the championship, their mother gave a party to celebrate their conquest of the title. Ermínio heard about it and went to his sister's house. He drank, sang, and joked with the girls as he always did. He danced with a few of them and also with Iraíldes. When they were dancing, she said she was going home.

"I'll take you," he said.

He had been attracted to her serious manner in the midst of the students' frivolity and wanted to know her better. He took her home, and they talked and soon began dating. Iraíldes went with him to his parties and gatherings, always behaving discreetly while Ermínio joked with everyone, laughed, told stories, and talked loudly. On the Sunday that he was twenty-eight years old, they spent the day going to the houses of relatives and friends, to a barbecue, and finally to a nightclub to dance. When Ermínio laid his face against hers, he was surprised to find it very hot. He drew away and in the flashing of the lights saw that her eyes were bright and feverish.

"Why, you're burning up with fever," he said.

"It's a cold," she explained.

"But why didn't you tell me?"

"I was fine, it only got worse this afternoon."

She had endured feeling miserable without saying one word.

"You were having so much fun and I didn't want to be a wet blanket."

Ermínio was most impressed with her attitude of consideration and unselfishness and they got engaged. After they were married Iraíldes kept on going with him to parties and bars, but after she got pregnant and their son was born, she stopped going out at night almost altogether. Ermínio didn't change his habit of talking and drinking with friends until the wee hours. Three years after their first son was born Iraíldes got pregnant again and had Thais, a girl with black eyes and a round face. Iraíldes no longer went out with Ermínio at all, and she started to complain, saying that he ought to change his ways. But he didn't. One day she followed him to the door, criticizing.

"A married man with children enjoys himself at home."

He was already halfway to the gate, but he stopped, waiting for her to finish speaking, and looked at an azalea she had transplanted a few days ago. He commented,

"There's no sun here, you should have put this someplace else."

"I can't believe it!" cried Iraíldes angrily. "Our marriage is falling apart and you talk about azaleas?"

She strode back inside the house and he went to meet his friends. He knew that she would never go beyond that point, never do more than nag. Another time, on a Saturday night, they had gone to a birthday party for another teacher in the parochial school and twice Iraíldes had suggested that it was time to leave. Ermínio ignored her suggestions. As usual, he felt quite at home. He was the center of attention, and he told stories and jokes, making everyone laugh and prolonging the party until the wee hours. When they got home, Ermínio singing and half-tipsy, she made him sit down in the kitchen while she made him some black coffee because, according to Iraíldes, if he didn't drink some coffee he would be in no condition to take her and the children on an outing they had planned for the next day. She waited for the water to boil, complaining about how long they had stayed at her friend's house and about him drinking and telling jokes until so late.

"Aren't you ever going to change?" she asked him.

She told him that he wasn't a young single man anymore, to be acting that way. That it wasn't fitting for her, a teacher, to have a husband who carried on like that at parties, laughing the loudest, telling the most jokes, drinking more than anyone else.

"And surrounding yourself with girls, as if you weren't the father of a family, with two children!"

Ermínio was drowsing over the table and she was standing at the stove, waiting for the water to boil, scolding him and pointing out what was wrong. At times she said, "Don't fall asleep, listen to what I'm saying."

"All right," he would answer, forcing his eyes to stay open. Seven-year-old Edgar, their oldest, woke up and wandered to the door of the kitchen in his pajamas, where he stood watching them.

Iraíldes sent him back to his room but he didn't budge from the spot. She was talking about Ermínio's having agreed to tell a particular joke, and demanded, "Why should a busybody like Thelma know what jokes you tell?"

He started falling asleep and she said, "Don't drop off, you still have to drink this coffee."

When the water boiled, she made a large cup of black coffee and gave it to him without sugar.

"I'm not going to drink that," Ermínio warned her when he tasted it. "It's awful."

"Oh, yes, you are."

"No, I'm not."

"Yes you are, too, or else we won't be able to go out tomorrow."

"I'm going to bed," he said, putting the coffee cup on the table.

"Ermínio, I still have a lot of things to say to you."

"You've already said them all," he answered, getting up out of the chair.

Iraíldes insisted that he sit down again and drink the coffee. And she said, "We still have a lot to discuss."

He got all the way up and she yelled, "Ermínio, please listen to me!"

Then he took the coffee cup and threw it on the floor. "What's this!" she cried. He reached for a tray full of glasses and overturned it as well. He took the plates, cups, and platters off the shelves and threw them all onto the floor. Iraíldes ran out of the kitchen into the living room, watching in horror. Ermínio broke everything, and when he finished he saw Edgar bending over near the door to pick up a glass that was still in one piece.

"This one didn't break, Dad," he said, handing it to him.

Ermínio took the glass and threw it onto the floor again, smashing it into a thousand pieces. Then he walked out of the kitchen, picking his way through the shards and bumping against the walls and table.

Iraíldes said from the living room, "Wait, you forgot the water filter."

Ermínio turned around, saw the china filter, and replied, "No, not it. It gives me water in the mornings after I've been out drinking."

As he left the kitchen he said to Edgar. "If she cleans this up, you help her, all right?"

"All right," Edgar agreed.

"I'm not cleaning up anything," Iraíldes announced.

Ermínio turned to his son again and explained, "So don't help her, all right?"

"Sure," Edgar agreed again.

Ermínio went across the living room in the direction of the bedroom and met Thais. She had been wakened by the crashing and banging and was up, rubbing her eyes.

"What is it?" he asked her.

"All that noise, Daddy," the girl answered.

He bent over to pick her up but saw that he might lose

his balance. Straightening up again, he took her by the hand and said, "It wasn't anything, Mayonnaise."

When he wanted to treat her very affectionately, he would call her Mayonnaise. Before she was born, Edgar had said that if the baby was a girl, Mayonnaise would be the best name. Ermínio thought it was very funny but Iraíldes didn't care for it a bit. Edgar was convinced it was a beautiful name and for some time was disgusted that they had called her Thais. That night, taking her by the hand, Ermínio called her Mayonnaise and took her to his bedroom.

"You can sleep with Daddy," he said.

Iraíldes stayed in the living room, looking at the mess in the kitchen, and then said to Edgar, "And you, what are you doing up at this hour? Straight to bed!"

As he went to lie down she went after him, and she could see Ermínio and their daughter already sound asleep, snoring. She went to bed in Thais's room but it took her a long time to fall asleep. The next morning she was awakened by Ermínio calling her to get ready for their outing.

"I'm leaving you," she said as she saw him come into the bedroom.

"All right," he said. "We'll discuss it later. Now let's get ready to go."

Iraíldes emphasized that she was quite serious.

"All right," repeated Ermínio. "We'll talk about it when we get back."

The whole time they were out together, he acted as if nothing had happened the night before. When they got home, he and Edgar cleaned up everything in the kitchen, while Thais, seated on a chair, warned them if they missed any slivers of glass or china. Iraíldes, in keeping with her promise, didn't lift a finger to help them. She sat in the living room with her arms crossed, watching the three in the kitchen chatting and perfectly content.

That night she slept in Thais's room again and once more stated, "Ermínio, I'm leaving you."

"Don't say that, sweetheart," he entreated.

"I'm serious. I've decided. I can't live with you anymore." And she asked him to please leave the room.

Ermínio went out pretending to be upset, but in reality his anxiety was not too great. He knew Iraíldes well enough to realize that it would take more than small exaggerations at parties or even a few bouts of china smashing to make her admit publicly that their marriage had failed.

Two other streets gave onto the square where Ermínio and Iraíldes lived and where the Santa Rita Church stood. Their names were Iguatama Street and Campo Alegre Street. On Campo Alegre lived a boy called Benício, who one day decided to raise rabbits. He asked his father, Sr. Elias, for part of the money, and also his mother, Dona Vânia. He sold empty bottles, offered to wash the neighbor's cars, and managed to get enough money to buy a pair of rabbits from another boy called Noah, who had been raising them for a while and had convinced him to start breeding them himself. After he got the two rabbits, Benício built a little hutch, closed in the surrounding area with bamboo and pieces of board, and put the rabbits inside. He took good care of them, never letting them go without food or water. They started to multiply quickly and the work increased. Benício began to lose his enthusiasm. He got tired of changing the water, finding lettuce and carrots, discovering the kind of grass they liked, and cleaning up after them. Dona Vânia wasn't fond of animals and complained of the smell they made in the backyard. One night there was a storm, with hard rain and wind. Several tiles from the hutch roof came loose and fell down, killing some of the rabbits. The maid told them about it when she found them dead in the morning. Dona Vânia felt sorry for the rabbits and their young that had been crushed by the falling tiles. She made Benício give up his rabbit raising; he was to sell the animals or give them away.

"I don't want the creatures around anymore," she said.

He gave some away, sold others, and the rabbits were reduced to only one couple, a male and a female. Both were large and entirely white. The female was sterile, and they ran loose in the backyard. They came into the house, hopped about the kitchen and living room, went into the street outside. They were pets. But once when they went out onto the front sidewalk, the female disappeared. She never came back, and the male was left all alone. Not long afterward, he hopped from the garage wall onto the car and miscalculated the distance, hit his head on the bumper, and died. Doris, Benício's sister, propounded the theory that he had committed suicide out of love, killing himself because he missed his companion. She would even argue about it, calling her brother to witness to the fact that animals commit suicide just like people.

A few doors down was the Confidence notions-and-paper shop, which belonged to Sr. Irineu Maia. In the afternoon, when there were fewer customers, he would come outside the shop to play dominoes with Sr. Nogueira, a retired man who had been director of the city band and lived across the street. Irineu would set out two chairs, and Sr. Nogueira would bring the domino set and a little table. They would play under a big tree that grew in front of the shop. If anyone wanted to buy something, they would shout, "Oh, Irineu!" and he would interrupt the game, attend the customer and come back. But during decisive moments, he wouldn't stop playing. He would motion to the customer to wait or, at times, depending on the person, tell them to go inside, choose what they wanted, and bring him the money. On one occasion when they were playing, the maid who worked for Dona Delise, Sr. Nogueira's neighbor, came across the street toward them, shouting. Irineu saw Sr. Nogueira get up from his chair and run behind the tree.

The maid had a butcher knife in one hand and a metal ornament in the other. She was screaming, "I'll kill that old man yet!"

Sr. Nogueira was skinny and Ireneu had never seen him run so fast. The maid began to chase him around the tree.

"I'll kill you this very day, you old codger!" she was shouting, clutching the knife and the ornament, unable to catch him.

Sr. Nogueira ran around the tree a few times, then ran into the notions store and slammed the door after him. The maid began beating on the door with the metal ornament.

"I'll kill you, you gossiping old bastard!"

Much surprised, Irineu was wondering what to do when Dona Delise came out of her house and crossed the street, calling to the maid.

"Stop that, Luisa. Can't you see that it isn't his fault?"

Luisa was swearing at Sr. Nogueira, shouting for him to open the door, and vowing to kill him because he had made her lose her job. "All I have in the world is this job!" she screamed.

Dona Delise came closer and said, "Here, stop that." She ordered the girl to go back to her house, taking her by the arm with no fear of the knife or the metal ornament. The two of them crossed the street and Irineu called to Sr. Nogueira to let him know he could come out now. He had to call more than once to get him to open the door.

"Got away by the skin of your teeth, eh?" he said.

Sr. Nogueira verified with relief that Luisa was really gone. "That girl is crazy," he remarked.

She did things that were wrong and then tried to blame it on him when she got fired. He said he had only told Dona Delise that Luisa was letting people borrow her sheets and pillowcases.

"I saw her do it," he confirmed.

Dona Delise backed her car out of the garage and stopped under the tree. Luisa was sitting beside her.

"Sr. Nogueira, it wasn't your fault," she explained. "I'm sending her away because she doesn't follow my orders and she talks back to me far too much." It wasn't anything he had said. She knew that Luisa had taken the pillowcases for her sister to copy the embroidery pattern, but that didn't matter.

"I fired her because she isn't treating me as I like to be treated."

The girl disobeyed her orders and addressed her disrespectfully. Dona Delise was taking the girl to her sister's house to stay there and would explain to the sister why she had decided to fire her. With Luisa looking daggers at Sr. Nogueira, Dona Delise accelerated the car and drove off.

Down the street lived little Analuce, three years old, who received a baby chick as a favor at a birthday party. She brought it home and Eveline, her mother, explained that she mustn't squeeze it too hard.

"You have to hold him very carefully," she taught the girl. She showed her how, and Analuce took care of the chick, which became her friend. In no time at all it would follow her all over the house. Eveline made a small cloth sack for the chick to sleep in and one evening Analuce's father, Musso Garcia, came into his daughter's room and saw it hanging from the bedstead. He thought it odd, and when he touched it, the chick moved around inside it and cheeped. He went to look for his wife.

"Is Analuce sleeping with that bird hanging from the bed?"

"Yes, she doesn't want to be separated from it," answered his wife. "Why?"

Musso Garcia didn't like his daughter's attachment to the chick, but he accepted what the mother and girl had done together. Some time afterward they went to the home of Eveline's parents, and it rained hard while they were there. The chick, which by this time was a young fryer and often went out to peck in the dirt, got soaking wet and died of cold or, as Musso Garcia affirmed, "From excess care, to be excessively frank."

When they got back from her grandparents' house, Analuce went to look for the chicken and discovered it dead near the back door. Eveline saw her bend over beside the chicken and bring her hands to her stricken face. Though her mother tried to talk to her, Analuce wouldn't answer, she just kept crying without a word.

"Darling, he got soaking wet and it made him sick," Eveline tried to explain. "He probably would have died later anyway."

That didn't make Analuce's sadness any less, and the two put the chicken inside a shoe box and buried it in the garden. The next day, when Musso Garcia got home from work, he found his daughter squatting beside the place where they had buried the chicken, her arms crossed. She was very silent, looking at the grave. He picked her up and carried her into the house.

"Want to ride piggyback? Or go out with Daddy in the car? How about some ice cream?" he said, trying to cheer her up.

Eveline signaled him to put the girl down and, after she went away, told him, "All she needs is love. She's understanding about death for the first time."

Some days later, when Musso Garcia came home from work one afternoon, he found the two conversing. Analuce wasn't at all sad anymore. She was saying that she didn't want another little chick; she wanted a big strong hen. A hen that wasn't scared of anything, that would never die and could peck harder than any old wind or rain.

Next to Musso Garcia's house lived Romano, who was an engineer. Once he had suffered a terrible electric shock when he tried to lift a piece of plywood off the tube that carried concrete up to the second story of the small building he was constructing. When he lifted the sheet of plywood he touched the end of a live wire conducting three electrical phases and received the entire discharge. He fell over onto the tube. As he convulsed he could see the workers staring at him. He felt his fingers burning on the wire and saw the men standing there idiotically, watching the convulsions that were killing him.

I can't die this way, he thought to himself. Fighting to stay alive, he marshaled all the strength left in him, crying, "Get me out of here!"

Two men drew closer from the circle of workers and tried to pull him away, but they also received a heavy shock and drew back. Powerless to act, he saw the two withdraw, feeling his body entirely electrified and realizing that he was dying. He made a last try, a superhuman effort, bigger than any he had ever made, and managed to say again, "Get me out of here!"

Then one of the men lifted his pick and brought it down on the wire, severing it. Romano fell to the floor, breathing hard and recuperating, still surrounded by the ring of immobile faces, nobody remembering to throw the main switch off. The foreman came running up. He had realized what was happening from down below. When he got to the second story, he found Romano already sitting up, his body no longer writhing or trembling.

Soon Romano was going home, arriving earlier than usual, and his wife Diana was asking him, "Did you hear what happened to Sheila?"

He couldn't remember who Sheila was.

"The girl who works in the record shop."

"I don't know who you mean," he answered.

"Yes you do, that girl in the shop near the gas station."

Diana kept insisting, and he wanted to keep quiet. Not knowing who the girl was, but with a vague remembrance of a pretty, cheerful blonde whom he had seen a few times in a store on the corner.

"A tall blond girl, very well mannered," Diana went on.

She told him that the night before, when Sheila got home, she had found her brother fiddling with a shotgun. "And it went off, and the bullet went right through her heart."

She had run out with her hand to her chest and fallen down dead in the street.

"I heard about it this morning right after you left." Romano didn't say anything about the electric shock, he only said that he couldn't recall the girl and mentioned that he didn't want dinner.

"Did anything happen?" asked Diana.

"Nothing important," he replied. "A few problems on the site. I don't have much appetite."

She remarked that he was working too hard, that he needed to relax more, rest a little.

"All you think about is work. You should enjoy yourself once in a while."

His seven-year-old son was at the table doing his homework, surrounded by textbooks and notebooks.

Romano asked him, "Jason, want to go fishing?"

"Now?" asked the boy, surprised.

"Sure, now. Want to go?"

"From the riverbank or in a boat?" the boy wanted to know.

"From the bank," his father answered.

"Yes, but you know that I only catch little fish, don't

you?" said the son, adding in his precociously logical way, "I'm not a patient fisherman."

"That doesn't matter," Romano told him. "Let's go anyhow."

The two of them took their fishing rods to the riverbank, joining others who, alone or in small groups, were fishing along the bank just before nightfall.

Jason never kept his line in one place for very long and Romano, to satisfy him, would say every so often, "Let's try another place."

And they would go somewhere else. Romano caught a fish and let Jason take it off the hook and put it on the string he had brought in a knapsack. While his son was busy with the fish, he watched the lights coming on in the streets and houses. The waters reflected those closest to the river. A heron or two glided low, preparing for the night's rest. As you looked at the boats anchored some distance away, with the lamps shining on their poops and the motionless profiles of the fishermen, the river seemed calmer, more immense and eternal. Romano gazed at the streets near its edge and at the square where Reinish, the German, was sitting under a tree surrounded by his sheep. When Romano finished his engineering course and first came back to the city, he would often meet him there. They would talk, and Reinish would tell of his life and his research. He had come from Europe with his parents before he was ten years old, and at eighty-two he still had German citizenship because, on the four occasions when he applied for naturalization, they demanded that he annex to his application police records from all the places he had lived.

And he remarked, "How can I get a clean police record from a time when I was a minor?"

So he didn't send for the police records from his childhood town, refusing to request something officially impossible. He was a specialist in sugarcane and studied the species that could adapt themselves to the mountains. Now that his life was nearing its close, he had chosen to stay there. Every afternoon, he went to the square and sat down on the bench under the tree, and his sheep, which never left him, spread themselves around him. He would sit on the bank watching the sun set, alone or conversing with someone, but always with the sheep nearby. He had acquired these sheep shortly after moving to the city and building the house where he lived. A friend of his named Bebeto had invited him to a barbecue. When Bebeto tried to slaughter a sheep from his herd, it escaped, running between his legs and causing him to fall onto the knife he was using. He hurt himself seriously.

While he was still in bed recovering, a sorceress told him, "Someone cast a spell to hurt you."

According to the woman, all his sheep had been put under the spell and represented a danger to him. Bebeto didn't believe the sorceress, but after a few days he told his wife to get rid of the sheep. She tried to find somebody to buy them and told Reinish that if nobody was interested, she was going to have them all slaughtered. Reinish bought them and turned them out into the large area behind his house. His friend no longer visited him, but in the afternoons when he went out, the sheep went with him.

Romano watched as night fell over the city and the river. Jason said, "Let's go home, Dad."

They left the riverbank and went into a bar where Romano had a beer and Jason some fruit juice. A man who was drinking at the counter greeted Romano.

"Good evening, sir."

"Good evening," he answered.

They went home. He and Jason ate the fish they had caught, and that night, after Diana fell asleep, Romano got up and went to the veranda. He turned on the lights that illuminated the yard and stood there looking at the well-clipped grass and the white metal tables and chairs that he always liked to have in his yard. He thought about his wife's long hair and how frightened he was that Diana would cut it. This wasn't any sort of sexual fetish, because his three-year-old daughter, Ursula, also had long hair, and he asked Diana not to cut it either. After giving her a bath Diana complained of the time it took to comb out and dry, and Ursula always cried because it tangled. But he made it very clear that he wouldn't be pleased if they wore their hair shorter. Out on the veranda, due to some combination of memories or associations he couldn't fathom, he realized for the first time that the white lawn furniture and the long hair represented ways of keeping his childhood away from him. They hid the vision of his mother curved over an iron table that held a sewing machine. Though still young, her hair was cropped short, and she was forever bent over the black iron table—a table that separated her from him and his brothers. Apparently in some corner of his mind there existed a need to deny that childhood sight. It represented a period he had always tried to erase from his memory.

Next to the house of the engineer Romano was the corner where Flower Street and Raimundo Mourão Street came together. On this corner, one day at 7:45 in the morning, City Mayor Brígido Tinoco caught sight of his ex-wife, Edna Marta. She worked in an educational-supply post run by the Ministry of Education. At that moment she was on her way to work. They had been separated for two years and Brígido Tinoco made an effort to see as little of her as possible. He avoided the streets she normally used when the supply post opened or closed, but that day he got involved in a conversation with Dona Cleusa and had to spend twenty minutes standing there. Edna Marta was on the opposite side of the street. Dona Cleusa was going on and on about a petition she had sent to the Municipal Council over a month ago. Nothing had been done about it.

"I did just as you told me," she was saying. "I got the signatures, followed the legal protocol, but up to now nothing has happened. It hasn't even been discussed!"

She told him how hard it had been to get the ninety-seven signatures. Everybody complained that the street needed paving, especially during the rainy season when it was nothing but mud. But when it came to getting a petition signed, they couldn't be bothered, nobody had time. Worse yet, she had left the list with certain people so they could sign it and pass it on, and they got the paper all dirty. Sr. Dario's wife actually sent the list back torn from top to bottom, and it had already been signed by twenty-two people. "She said it was her son who tore it. But she didn't go after the twenty-two signatures, I had to get them all over again, one by one."

Brígido Tinoco was listening attentively when he saw his ex-wife come up the street toward the supply post from her mother's house. He stood there hearing Dona Cleusa out and watching Edna Marta clutch her purse in front of her body as if defending herself from the cold. She had acquired that habit as a young girl. During the months of May and June she and her classmates hid their breasts when they came outside in the morning to go to school. They hugged their school bags in front of them because the cold wind made their nipples erect and the boys and old men would notice and make jokes. Brígido looked at his ex-wife and remembered the children they had had. They were born apparently healthy and perfect, but all dead. Three deliveries, three dead babies. After the second the doctor advised them not to try again because they would probably have their hopes dashed once more.

"It's almost zero, Dona Edna, the possibility of your bearing a live child."

But she stubbornly tried, believing it was possible and getting pregnant for the third time. The third child was born dead, too. There were complications, a cesarean section was necessary, and Brígido was in the middle of his election campaign. All his time was taken up with meetings and political rallies. He was only there to attend the funeral. The funeral of a child who, like the others, had never really existed. Immediately afterward he had to travel to outlying districts and his sister, Helenice, and Dona Silvia, Edna Marta's mother, stayed at the hospital to keep her company. Helenice stayed at night and Dona Silvia during the day. Afterward Edna Marta remarked what a good, reliable friend Helenice was: solid, calm, always there when she was needed. That first night Edna Marta felt profoundly depressed and cried for hours on end, relieving herself of some of her pain and despair. Helenice didn't wake up at all, but lay quietly in the bed next to hers.

The next morning, seeing Edna Marta's pensive face, Helenice asked, "Do you feel better now?"

She had been aware of all the crying, but had stayed quiet just to leave Edna Marta in peace, not to invade her privacy. Brígido Tinoco also remembered Edna's times of pregnancy. In spite of her worries, she felt fine. She would pull him over so he could put his hand on her belly and say that if she had been born a slave woman, she would have been happy to bear children one after another.

"I'd like to have babies all the time."

She dreamed of nursing the baby, changing diapers, giving baths. After their separation Brígido avoided meeting her. He avoided the streets she followed when she went to work. That morning, seeing her climb uphill across the street from him, he interrupted what Dona Cleusa was saying.

"I'll look into it this very day, ma'am, and see why it hasn't been put on the agenda," he said. "I promise that I'll find a solution by the end of the week."

He said good-bye, but instead of getting into the car and going to his office, he went across the street to meet his ex-wife. As she approached he saw that she wore no earrings or necklace and that her hair was unkempt, her sandals worn. When she saw him, she smiled, uncrossed her arms, and smoothed down her collar, patting a lock of hair that had fallen over her forehead into place. They greeted each other, and Edna seemed pleased to see him. They went on up the street and Brígido noted that Edna Marta wasn't wearing the watch he had given her as a gift for the first year they had known each other. She saw him looking and said she had borrowed her mother's watch.

"Mine isn't running right and I haven't had time to take it to the repairman."

She mentioned how long it took her to get to work and that at night sometimes her legs ached.

"I walk this distance four times a day and on the job I stand up all the time."

He advised her to prop her feet up when she got home and told her he had very little free time himself. So many people came to see him, asking favors, wanting things he had promised. "And most of them aren't even in my constituency."

"But you're doing fine, anyone can see," she commented, gazing into his face.

He smiled and said that she was looking well herself.

"No, I'm not," Edna Marta answered. "And you know it."

As they approached the supply post they met a man who was driving two donkeys loaded down with bananas.

"Ouuu . . . git up there!" the man called to the donkeys.

They stopped, and the man came to a halt beside Brígido.

"Sr. Mayor, can I have a word with you, sir?"

Brígido asked him to wait a minute and said to Edna, "You go on, I'll stay here."

"All right," she answered. "It was nice to see you."

"Nice to see you, too," he said. He felt like kissing her on the face but contained himself. She walked off and he asked the man, "So, Sr. Duca, what can I do for you?"

The man began to speak. Brígido listened to his problem as he followed his ex-wife with his eyes. She pretended not to notice. When she reached the building where she worked, she turned around, saw that he was still there, and smiled as she went inside. Brígido heard the man telling him that his oldest daughter, a girl of eleven, had a very high fever. She had gone to the government health clinic twice but hadn't improved.

"She took the medicine but it didn't help."

"Take her to the clinic again and ask the doctor about it," Brígido advised.

"But she's too weak to walk now, Sr. Mayor." And he couldn't bring her on one of the donkeys because they weren't trained to be ridden.

"Do you remember the name of the doctor who attended your daughter?"

The man told him the doctor's name. Brígido wrote it down, along with Sr. Duca's name, on a piece of paper and sent him to the medical post to search for the doctor.

"Go over there right away and talk to him. Tell him she can't get out of bed."

Sr. Duca went on his way and Brígido started toward the corner where he had left his car. But shortly he stopped beside a little girl, the daughter of a beggarwoman. Once he had given her a doll. She was playing with it now and her mother, who begged on the sidewalks, sent her to ask the mayor for his blessing. The girl raised her eyes, smiled at Brígido, and ran to kiss his hand. He patted her head and she went back to the wall where she had propped the doll. The major continued toward the corner of Raimundo Mourão Street. He exchanged greetings with several people and noticed the accumulation of rubbish in two vacant lots. He knew that the garbage-collection service wasn't running properly. The truck only passed by on Mondays and Thursdays, and they needed to deal with this problem, to find a way of annulling the contract the city had made with Sr. Djalma, owner of the truck. It wouldn't be easy because Sr. Djalma was in business with Márcio Lírio, a popular and influential councilman. They didn't want the contract changed because on the other days of the week, they used the truck to transport sand from the riverbank and sell to construction companies. If Brígido were to propose any modification, the councilman would discourse lengthily, insinuate dishonesty on Brígido's part, and there would be no way to prove that he and Sr. Djalma were partners. The truck belonged to both of them but there were no papers signed. As he noticed the rubbish and worried about how to change the contract, Brígido Tinoco looked toward General Faraco Square, where rainwater always collected, creating a constant problem. It had started when the Brazilian army had chosen to donate a statue to the city and cement the square over. The statue was a bust of some heroic general in the Paraguayan War who had no descendants in the town. Nobody there knew his story, but the army promoted celebrations and speeches in his honor and installed the bust in the middle of the square after covering the latter over with cement. After that it was constantly necessary to break the cement during the rainy season to uncover drainholes and let the water run off.

"A native son who became a hero long ago and is only remembered for the problems he brought to his town," Brígido had commented more than once to the vice-mayor.

As he walked toward the car his progress was once again interrupted by a very nervous man who said that his sister's clothes had disappeared in the charity hospital.

"She stayed there for three days, Sr. Mayor. She died and they gave me her body this morning, but without a stitch on."

They had released the body covered only by a sheet. His sister had gone to the charity hospital wearing a skirt, a blouse, a warm jacket, and shoes.

"They stole all her clothes!" he said. "And shoes, too!" He had protested, but nobody in the charity hospital had been able to help him. He explained that he was the nephew of Dona Gercina, an old neighbor of Brígido's mother.

"Oh, I remember, a very dear lady," said Brígido Tinoco. And he advised the man to go to the police and tell them what had happened.

"But I already spoke to the officer at the door of the hospital and he didn't do a thing."

"No, no, go down to the station. Look for the sheriff. Explain to him that you spoke to me and that I sent you there."

The man went off, and before Brígido could open his car door, he heard someone else calling him. It was a man named Cleto who used to work as a chauffeur for the city. He had resigned from his job and moved to São Paulo.

"You're back?" asked Brígido.

"I came to see about some things, Sr. Mayor."

He was in town to sell a piece of his late wife's land, which his brothers-in-law had been renting from him for pasture.

"But did your wife pass away?" asked Brígido, surprised.

"Yes, she did, Sr. Mayor. She couldn't adjust to São Paulo. She got sick and went from bad to worse until there was nothing more to be done, poor thing," answered the former chauffeur.

Brígido thought about the times he and Edna had talked about Cleto. Everyone knew how badly he treated his wife.

"He's mean to her but he doesn't have the courage to beat her," Brígido would say to Edna Marta. "He's afraid of her brothers."

There were four brothers, all very tough men. They rented his wife's land for pasture.

"Cleto's scared of them, and there's the money she gets from the land, too."

When Edna Marta heard that they were moving to São Paulo, she asked, "Do you suppose that once he gets her away from her brothers he'll actually beat her?"

"He'll end up killing her and coming back here to get the money from her land," Brígido had commented, more or less jokingly. Now here was Cleto telling him that his wife had died. It certainly was a disagreeable coincidence.

"Or else I had a premonition," he concluded to himself.

Cleto told him about the diseases his wife had had in São Paulo, and how he had done everything to keep her from dying. Brígido listened to his explanations and thought about the comments Edna would make if she knew.

"If I ever need help, I'll look you up, Sr. Mayor," Cleto said as he finished his story.

"By all means," answered Brígido. He got into the car and drove away, wishing he could talk with Edna and tell her of the coincidence or confirmation of what they had said more than two years ago. Being unable to exchange ideas with her and comment on the things he experienced or heard about was what made the separation hardest. He had gotten into the habit of talking exclusively about his own problems and interests while she unfailingly gave him her attention.

"Very selfish of me," he recognized. "Always, very selfish."

He recognized that their relationship had always been like that. Though he had been concerned only with his political interests, she had accepted him that way. He thought about this there in the car and also thought about the impossibility of accepting her back as she had accepted him countless times.

"Not accepting her, isn't that just a convenient attitude, really?" he had sometimes asked himself.

"Not in this case," he answered. "In this case it's the consequence of my upbringing." In the long nights of solitude he had concluded, "Values were implanted in me that don't permit me to have her back. To accept her I would have to make a superhuman effort." An effort beyond his abilities, at least at this point in his life, as he told himself.

He remembered Edna Marta's words.

"But, Brígido, you're the man I love. I wouldn't trade you for anyone, don't you see that?"

He did. She didn't play games, plan her acts, divide the world into what was right or wrong according to her interests as he had a tendency to do.

"Then why did you let him hold you and kiss you?"

"I don't know," she answered. "I was depressed,

drowning in thoughts of discouragement that made me sad. And you were always away."

He knew she was sincere, not only from the years they had spent together, but also from what he had learned to identify in people's words.

"You were always busy with your own affairs, far away, and he was there—permanent, close, attentive. I felt I could lean on him; he helped me. When he came close and took me in his arms, I didn't mind. I didn't feel offended. That physical contact did me good."

He listened without anger, without resentment.

"It did me good, but it didn't mean I was really attracted to him, it took nothing away from what I felt, and still feel, for you," Edna told him. "I wouldn't trade you for him or for anyone, ever, you know that. These things a person just knows."

And she repeated, "I didn't want to hurt you." It had happened very naturally, just a friendly person coming closer. "I don't really know why I didn't resist." And she repeated, "I miss you and cry at night because of what happened. And I know you're suffering, too. But tell me, what am I to do?"

The sight of the other man holding her, turning her face to him and kissing her. Edna receiving the kiss without moving, not drawing away, not repelling him. This sight was impossible for him to blot out. There were barriers profoundly rooted in his being that kept him from forgiving that image. Now he thought of Edna's appearance that morning when they met: scruffy hair, worn-out shoes. The signs of suffering in her face and eyes. Signs of the process that he had foreseen from the beginning and that were confirmed each time he met her. The truth was, he loved her. He loved and respected that woman.

"But how can I get rid of the values that were cultivated in me?" he asked himself.

So on that morning Brígido Tinoco arrived at his office in the city building thinking these things. It was a low, handsome building, close to the house where Jaime Albano, the doctor, lived. Jaime's wife, Aurea, immediately after giving birth to a child, would place it naked on her body. She would nurse the babies anywhere if they happened to be hungry. She went about it with such a natural air that he accepted her taking out her breast in public and offering it to the baby. Jaime Albano slept lightly, accustomed as he was to being awakened at night, and as soon as he fell asleep he heard the doorbell ring.

Someone was calling, "Dr. Jaime! Dr. Jaime!"

He got up without waking Aurea, put on a bathrobe, and went to the window. It was Dona Dilma's youngest son.

"Doctor, Mother's very bad off."

"I'm on my way," he said.

He closed the window and got dressed quickly without turning on the light, grabbed his medical bag, and went out, leaving Aurea sound asleep. As he opened the garage door he saw that the night had grown colder. He got in the car and, as he passed the pickup truck driven by Dona Dilma's son, heard him beg, "Come as fast as you can, Doctor."

"You follow me," said Jaime.

At that time of night, they would reach the ranch in thirty minutes if they drove fast. Dona Dilma and her husband, Sr. Varela, were heart patients, though she presented more serious symptoms of coronary obstruction. Jaime sped down the road, which was entirely deserted at that hour, and saw the pickup's headlights in the rearview mirror, now coming closer, now falling behind. At times they almost disappeared in the darkness of the night. At the ranch the lights of the house were on and from the veranda one could hear people crying in the living room. Dona Dilma had already died. When he went in, her body was still in an armchair with Sr. Varela standing beside it. In a corner two servants were crying. When he saw the doctor, Sr. Varela went to meet him, explaining what had happened. He was unwilling to accept that Dona Dilma was really dead and talked as though to convince himself that it was just another bad spell.

"We were talking, Doctor, and she stopped answering. Then she put her hand up to her chest."

The son who had come to fetch him went over to the mother's body and began to cry, too. Sr. Varela explained that when he saw Dilma holding her chest, he yelled for Fabiano, the only unmarried son, who was still living with them.

"I sent him running to get you, Doctor."

He said that Dilma had difficulty breathing and appeared to be in a lot of pain. Then her effort stopped.

"And she stayed just as she is, Doctor."

She was sixty-eight years old and quite fat. Sr. Varela was seventy-four. He kept saying, "Poor Dilma."

The other sons and the daughter-in-law were arriving and more people began to cry. Jaime made Sr. Varela sit down in a chair and explained that his wife was dead. Then, with the help of the sons, he carried her body to the bedroom.

As they lifted it she seemed to sigh and Sr. Varela exclaimed, disoriented, "Look, Doctor, she's breathing!"

Jaime explained to him that she wasn't breathing, it had been the air that was still in her lungs. Sr. Varela began to cry, to realize that she was indeed gone. He started to help carry the body.

But he went in the direction of the bathroom instead, came back before using it, and repeated, "Poor Dilma."

Jaime didn't give him a sedative. He judged that due to his cardiac instability, it was better to leave him as he was: surrounded by the children, relatives, and friends who were arriving.

"It's going to be hard for him," he told the sons.

They were all in a state of confusion, and Jaime explained what they should do in order for the body to be buried. He gave instructions as to how to care for Sr. Varela, handed them the certificate of death, and said good-bye. He liked the couple and had foreseen Dona Dilma's passing as he foresaw the few years that were left to Sr. Varela. As he left the ranch a few birds were already singing, and he identified the melancholy whistle of a thrush.

Sr. Varela's last years will be sad ones, he thought to himself inside the car.

He didn't go back to bed when he got home, just took a shower, shaved, and had some coffee and breakfast with Aurea, commenting vaguely about last night's activities. It was still early when he went to the small hospital. When he arrived, he met Dulce in the waiting room. She came once a week for her exams and the other things necessary to control her diabetes. She was waiting to be called and he greeted her. A young woman, she was dressed as usual in expensive, well-made clothes. Today she wore a shade of blue that went well with her blond hair and green eyes. They exchanged a few words and he went down the hallway. She was taking the treatment seriously, different from a short while ago when she didn't follow the diet, rules, or prescriptions, as if they were necessary only for other people. Not for her, accustomed to seeing her father's money and power remove disagreeable circumstances from her path. Then she had the crisis, and when she questioned him, he explained everything carefully, reaffirming the necessity for treatment, telling her clearly about her state of health. Then, only then, did she understand the consequences of not following his orders. Her green eyes filled with tears and she began to cry.

"But this can't be happening to me!" she said.

She no longer looked at him as though wanting to seduce a man whose word had the power to change people's fate. Her eyes wandered over the walls of the room as she repeated, "This can't be happening to me."

Finally she focused on him, seeing only someone able to help her control her illness. No longer the magician, the infallible source of wisdom. Dulce became a conscientious patient, participating in and cooperating with her treatment. Jaime had had a similar experience with another patient, Sr. Zenóbio. But his case left the doctor feeling less comfortable. Later he had been assaulted by doubts and uncertainty. Zenóbio went into the hospital without a chance of recovery. There was no possibility of checking the rapid spread of cancer, and Jaime sought instead to diminish his suffering and pain.

Zenóbio was always impatient, irritable. He swore at the nurses and hospital attendants. He complained about the uncomfortable positions and told them all how bad he felt, saying that the nurses were to blame and calling them incompetent. He protested how long it took for the painkillers to work, claiming, "They're not giving me the right medicines."

He said that the herbs and roots on his ranch didn't make him suffer that way. He would hardly let the nurses and attendants into his room. Jaime was worried. After exchanging ideas with another doctor and a priest, he decided to talk frankly with Zenóbio. He sat down near his bed and listed to his complaints, letting him curse everything and everyone. After Zenóbio had had his say, Jaime spoke with him, explaining that no one was to blame for his pain, not the nurses, the hospital, or even the doctors. It was due to his disease, which was advancing.

"It's a very serious disease, Sr. Zenóbio."

They had done all that was possible.

"We've tried everything. There's nothing more we can do." He talked to him not as a doctor, but as a man sharing another man's burden. Zenóbio listened and kept quiet. Jaime said that he would be at his disposal for whatever he wished.

"You have only to call me, anytime, and I'll be here."

Sr. Zenóbio didn't answer. He remained silent, and from then on he neither complained nor accepted any more medication. Three days later he died, without permitting the nurses to lessen his suffering. He wouldn't take any painkillers at all.

That day, after talking to Dulce and remembering Sr. Zenóbio, Jaime thought again about Dona Dilma and Sr. Varela. He remembered them waiting for him on the veranda of their farmhouse when he made visits. He struggled to convince them to change their eating habits, to be less sedentary. He remembered the couple telling him of the victory they had achieved, a fifteen-minute walk, and how they were managing to put only a tiny bit of butter on their toast, though he knew they still ate cake made with so many eggs. Jamie liked them both, and the loneliness that would envelop Sr. Varela in his last years of life made him sad.

There in the hospital Dr. Jaime went on examining his patients, talking with them one by one, prescribing medicines. Walking between the beds of the infirmary, asking the man called Pericles if his shaking had lessened. Pericles had given up alcohol but he still jerked and trembled so badly that sometimes they had to tie him into bed. The leather strips were still holding down his arms and legs, passing over his abdomen, his chin.

"Were you very agitated last night?"

"I was, Doctor, but I won't jump anymore."

"For sure?"

"You can untie me, I won't jump."

"Do you still think the building is falling?"

"Yes, I do, Doctor, but even so I won't jump again. I promise."

Jaime said he would tell them to unbuckle him.

"Before lunch I'll stop by, and if you're not worked up, I'll tell them to remove the straps."

"I won't get out of bed, I promise. The ceiling can fall in on me but I won't jump to either side."

The other patients paid no attention to Pericles and Jaime's conversation.

"Look, the building isn't falling down, it's being repaired. A small part is undergoing renovation."

"That's just it, Doctor, they're doing this renovation all wrong, because the place is on the brink of falling."

Jaime stopped beside the bed of Sr. Hugo, a terminal patient.

"Did you sleep better last night, Sr. Hugo?"

On the little cupboard near the bed was the plastic strip with piano keys where he practiced portions of music. He would open the "keyboard" on his lap and play on the imaginary piano, registering the notes as he composed on lined paper that was kept inside the cupboard. He experimented on the keyboard and heard the sounds in his mind. Examining him daily, Jaime confirmed the steady worsening of his liver condition. They discussed composing music. Sr. Hugo would tell him about the latest ideas he had come up with. He would show him what he had composed the day before, and Jaime would concentrate in an attempt to identify the sounds that would come out if the keyboard were real. He admired the musician, the most seriously ill of his patients and the most tranquil. Knowing that it was impossible to realize his project but not defeated. He didn't allow himself to be discouraged in the face of anything, but continued to compose in spite of his poverty, his incurable disease, and the short time he had left to live. He kept looking for solutions to the sonata he would never finish.

And when the floodgates of the dam were closed, the hospital, squares, roads, ranches, everything—Dr. Jaime's house, the other houses, everything was covered by the waters. All the places where those people had lived are now submerged forever in silence and darkness at the bottom of the lake.

TITLES OF THE AVAILABLE PRESS   *In order of publication*

THE CENTAUR IN THE GARDEN, a novel by Moacyr Scliar*
EL ANGEL'S LAST CONQUEST, a novel by Elvira Orphée
A STRANGE VIRUS OF UNKNOWN ORIGIN, a study by Dr. Jacques Leibowitch
THE TALES OF PATRICK MERLA, short stories by Patrick Merla
ELSEWHERE, a novel by Jonathan Strong*
THE AVAILABLE PRESS/PEN SHORT STORY COLLECTION
CAUGHT, a novel by Jane Schwartz*
THE ONE-MAN ARMY, a novel by Moacyr Scliar
THE CARNIVAL OF THE ANIMALS, short stories by Moacyr Scliar
LAST WORDS AND OTHER POEMS, poetry by Antler
O'CLOCK, short stories by Quim Monzó
MURDER BY REMOTE CONTROL, a novel in pictures by Janwillem van de Wetering and Paul Kirchner
VIC HOLYFIELD AND THE CLASS OF 1957, a novel by William Heyen*
AIR, a novel by Michael Upchurch
THE GODS OF RAQUEL, a novel by Moacyr Scliar*
SUTERISMS, pictures by David Suter
DOCTOR WOOREDDY'S PRESCRIPTION FOR ENDURING THE END OF THE WORLD, a novel by Colin Johnson
THE CHESTNUT RAIN, a poem by William Heyen
THE MAN IN THE MONKEY SUIT, a novel by Oswaldo França Júnior
KIDDO, a novel by David Handler*
COD STREUTH, a novel by Bamber Gascoigne
LUNACY & CAPRICE, a novel by Henry Van Dyke
HE DIED WITH HIS EYES OPEN, a mystery by Derek Raymond*
DUSTSHIP GLORY, a novel by Andreas Schroeder
FOR LOVE, ONLY FOR LOVE, a novel by Pasquale Festa Campanile
'BUCKINGHAM PALACE,' DISTRICT SIX, a novel by Richard Rive
THE SONG OF THE FOREST, a novel by Colin Mackay*
BE-BOP, RE-BOP, a novel by Xam Wilson Cartier
THE DEVIL'S HOME ON LEAVE, a mystery by Derek Raymond*
THE BALLAD OF THE FALSE MESSIAH, a novel by Moacyr Scliar
LITTLE PICTURES, short stories by Andrew Ramer
THE IMMIGRANT: A Hamilton County Album, a play by Mark Harelik
HOW THE DEAD LIVE, a mystery by Derek Raymond*
BOSS, a novel by David Handler*
THE TUNNEL, a novel by Ernesto Sábato
THE FOREIGN STUDENT, a novel by Philippe Labro, translated by William R. Byron
ARLISS, a novel by Llyla Allen
THE CHINESE WESTERN: Short Fiction From Today's China, translated by Zhu Hong
THE VOLUNTEERS, a novel by Moacyr Scliar
LOST SOULS, a novel by Anthony Schmitz
SEESAW MILLIONS, a novel by Janwillem van de Wetering
SWEET DIAMOND DUST, a novel by Rosario Ferré
SMOKEHOUSE JAM, a novel by Lloyd Little
THE ENIGMATIC EYE, short stories by Moacyr Scliar
THE WAY IT HAPPENS IN NOVELS, a novel by Kathleen O'Connor
THE FLAME FOREST, a novel by Michael Upchurch
FAMOUS QUESTIONS, a novel by Fanny Howe
SON OF TWO WORLDS, a novel by Haydn Middleton
WITHOUT A FARMHOUSE NEAR, by Deborah Rawson
THE RATTLESNAKE MASTER, by Beaufort Cranford

* Available in a Ballantine Mass Market Edition.